WHAT HE SAW

GLENN PARKER

Suite 300 - 990 Fort St
Victoria, BC, Canada, V8V 3K2
www.friesenpress.com

Copyright © 2019 by Glenn Parker
First Edition — 2019

All rights reserved.

No part of this publication may be reproduced in any form, or by
any means, electronic or mechanical, including photocopying,
recording, or any information browsing, storage, or retrieval
system, without permission in writing from the publisher.

ISBN
978-1-5255-4171-1 (Hardcover)
978-1-5255-4172-8 (Paperback)
978-1-5255-4173-5 (eBook)

Fiction, Coming Of Age

Distributed to the trade by The Ingram Book Company

THE ROAD NOT TAKEN

By Robert Frost

Two roads diverged in a yellow wood,
And sorry I could not travel both
And be one traveler, long I stood
And looked down one as far as I could
To where it bent in the undergrowth;

Then took the other, as just as fair,
And having perhaps the better claim,
Because it was grassy and wanted wear;
Though as for that the passing there
Had worn them really about the same,

And both that morning equally lay
In leaves no step had trodden black.
Oh, I kept the first for another day!
Yet knowing how way leads on to way,
I doubted if I should ever come back.

I shall be telling this with a sigh
Somewhere ages and ages hence:
Two roads diverged in a wood, and I—
I took the one less traveled by,
And that has made all the difference.

WHAT HE SAW

When I was twelve I spent a lot of time in my fort. I called it my fort, but it wasn't actually a fort. It was just a hidden spot amongst the trees where I could sit and look out across the water at the island. It's called Snake Island because it's supposed to have a whole lot of rattle snakes on it, but I've never been there so I don't know how true that is. I would like to have gone there sometime, but I don't have a boat and it was too far to swim, even if I could swim. But it would be interesting to see all those snakes. It would just be a matter of avoiding being bitten by one of them. I've got enough to think about without worrying about being bitten by a snake.

My name is Ryan Sinclair. I'm twelve years old and have the reddest hair ever known to mankind along with a galaxy of freckles. Every morning when I get up and look at myself in the mirror, I hope that maybe my hair has toned down a little bit, but that hasn't happened yet. I don't like standing out in a crowd, but with my hair being as bright as it is, it's hard to miss me. I told my mom that I was going to dye my hair black or at least some other less obvious color, but she was horrified.

"Your hair is beautiful just the way it is," she said. "Don't you even think about changing its color."

Spoken like a true mom, I thought. But I still hated my hair and all those freckles.

Getting back to my fort, anybody going by can't see me, but I can see them and that kind of made me feel like I had an advantage over them. Not that many people go by though. Where I was it is quite an isolated spot. Not many people know about it, but it was special to me. I could sit here and think about things without having to worry about Mrs. Johnson calling me to make sure I wasn't getting into trouble. Not that I was a trouble-maker or anything like that, but Mrs. Johnson figured she had to do her job and make sure she knew where I was every minute of the day. When she wasn't looking, I snuck out of the house and came here to my hideout. I could just picture her running around trying to find me. Good luck on that. I was miles away and the chances of her finding me were about as likely as the sun not rising the next morning. Mom hired Mrs. Johnson to look after us kids while she was at work. She didn't think that at twelve years old, I was old enough to look after myself and my two siblings. I liked calling my two sisters my siblings. It had a kind of nice ring to it. My grandma asked me one day if I knew what siblings were and when I shook my head, she explained that they were my brothers and sisters. Of course, I don't have a brother but sisters still counted as siblings I guess. They are both younger than me. Angela is only nine and a half and Sara is seven and they fight all the time. That's another reason why I liked coming here to my fort. I didn't have to listen to my sisters yelling at each other.

It was very peaceful at my fort. All I could hear were the birds chirping and the waves breaking against the rocks. It was real nice. Sometimes I just lay back and go to sleep, but most of the time I thought about things, like school and how much I hated it, and my two sisters who drove me crazy. My mom is nice though. I sometimes wonder how she could have had two daughters who were so obnoxious when she was so nice. My dad left us a long time ago, like a year or more, and we haven't seen or heard from him since. I guess he's gone for good, but maybe that was for the best. He didn't treat my mom very well and ignored me as though I was invisible. So, it's no big deal that he's gone. I missed not having a proper dad and doing things like going fishing or hiking, things like that. He could have taken me over to Snake Island sometime, but I guess that never occurred to him. Not many people go over there anyway. There's not much to see except all those rattle snakes. I was going to ask him if he could take me over sometime, but since we don't own a boat and also because he would have just looked at me as though I was crazy, I never did ask him.

I glanced at my watch. It was getting on to five o'clock and Mom would be coming home soon. I wanted to be there when she arrived so that Mrs. Johnson wouldn't be going ballistic about me being missing for a few hours. Mom was always very patient and rarely worried about me like Mrs. Johnson did.

I was just about to haul my bike out of my fort (there was enough room for both me and my bike) when I heard a car. Hardly anybody drove here. There is no proper road for one thing and when it rains, it gets pretty soggy and anybody in a car might get bogged down in the mud and get stuck. I waited until it passed, but unfortunately, it stopped and some guy got out and stood looking around as though he was lost or something. He was a tall guy with bushy light brown hair and a moustache dressed in one of those camouflage outfits that soldiers wear. At first, I thought he was by himself, maybe scouting out a place to play some wargames or something. But after looking around, at one point looking right in my direction, he opened the rear door of his car, reached in and pulled out a lady who was obviously asleep, put her on the ground and stood staring down at her. Then, after closing the rear door, he picked the lady up and started walking toward the trees.

I wondered what he was doing, but I didn't want to hang around to find out, so once he disappeared into the trees, I got out of there and headed for home. Of all the times I had spent in my fort, I had never seen anybody come there in a car. It seemed kind of crazy to me. And what had he intended to do with the lady he was carrying? That was even crazier.

3

All the way home, I kept thinking about the man and what he was up to. Maybe I should have stayed behind and found out, but I was too scared.

When I got home, Mom was already there and Mrs. Johnson had left, thank heavens. At least I wouldn't have to listen to her whine about me leaving without letting her know.

"Where have you been?" Mom asked when I came into the house. "Mrs. Johnson was very upset. She thought something might have happened to you."

"I was just…riding around on my bike," I told her.

Mom shook her head. "You should let Mrs. Johnson know when you plan to disappear like that. She's responsible for you and your sisters when I'm gone. I pay her good money to keep an eye on you."

"She probably wouldn't have let me go if I had asked her. It was just easier to take off without all the hassle."

"Come here," Mom said. She was sitting on the couch and patted the seat next to her. "I want to talk to you."

I hung up my coat and sauntered over to her and sat down. She looked really serious. What had I done that made her want to have a talk to me? It wasn't as though this was the first time I had ditched Mrs. Johnson.

Mom reached out and pushed the hair out of my eyes. "Now…surely you weren't riding around on your bike all that time. What were you doing?" I couldn't help smiling at my mom. She was so earnest.

"I…I was down at the beach."

"The beach? What were you doing there?"

"Just looking around. It's real nice down there. I like it and I like being by myself with nobody to bother me."

"Nobody to bother you?" My mom chuckled. "Now, who would bother you? There's just your sisters." She looked over at me. "You don't mean Mrs. Johnson, do you?"

I nodded. "She's always … telling me what to do. I'm twelve years old. I don't need somebody bossing me around all the time."

"Well, the summer holidays are almost over. Then you'll be back at school. You won't see Mrs. Johnson that often. But I can't understand why you don't like her. She's a very nice lady."

"No, she's not."

Mom laughed. "Well, I guess from your perspective she's not. But she's just trying to do her job. And it's not easy finding somebody to look after you and the girls." She heaved a sigh. "Promise me you'll try to get along with her."

I hated disappointing my mom. She probably had enough things on her plate without me acting like a spoiled brat.

"I saw something down at the beach," I suddenly said. I hadn't intended to tell Mom what I had seen, but the words just seemed to pop out of my mouth before I could stop myself.

"Just what did you see?" Mom looked worried again. Her blue eyes became even bluer as she stared at me as though I was about to reveal something catastrophic.

"I saw a man," I began. "He drove a car near my fort. Then he—" I stopped. Did I really want to worry my mom even more than she was already worried?

"You saw a man."

"What was he doing?"

"He…carried a lady into the trees. She was asleep I think. It kind of spooked me, so I got out of there and came home."

"He carried her into the trees? Ryan, what are you telling me? That she was dead, that he might have killed her?"

Mom looked so worried. I hated it when she looked at me the way she was looking now. What had I done? I took a deep breath. Somehow, I had to turn this whole thing around or else Mom would be going off the deep end. As if she didn't already have enough to worry about. Besides, it was probably nothing anyway.

"I think they were just fooling around," I said.

"Fooling around"? Mom stared at me for a long time and then started to laugh. "Just what do you know about "fooling around"?

I grinned at her and shrugged. I didn't mind looking like a dope if it meant Mom wasn't going to get all upset.

"It sounded a lot more serious than that," she said. "Are you sure about what you saw?"

"Yeah, I think they were just a couple of love birds, you know, looking for a place to…"

My mom laughed again. "Well, we won't go into that. Sometimes we see things we aren't sure about." She patted me on the head. "Now, I've got to get your dinner started. The girls are out on the patio playing a game. Maybe you want to join them."

I shook my head. That was something I definitely didn't want to do. "I think I'll clean up my room." I grinned at her, knowing full well that my gesture would make her day. Mom was easy to please. That was something I really liked about her.

She laughed. "The world is coming to an end. My son is going to clean up his room. Is the sky going to fall too?"

It was nice seeing my mom so happy. Cleaning up my room was my way of making up for being such a dipstick and causing her to worry unnecessarily. I felt protective of my mom since my dad had deserted us, just left without a word leaving mom to fend on her own and look after three kids. Not a nice prospect. Mom worked part time at a doctor's office as a receptionist. We could never have lived on what she brought home. Luckily, she had an inheritance from her parents which kept us from being poor.

When I got to my room, I sat down on the bed and looked around. The place was a mess. It really did need some cleaning, but for the moment, I didn't feel like doing anything. I kept thinking about that man who had carried the woman into the trees. It had spooked me more than I thought. There was just something about the whole thing that didn't seem quite right. Was it the way the man kept looking around as though worried about someone seeing him? I was glad I hadn't told Mom how I felt, how scared I was. I was quite sure that man wouldn't have been pleased if he knew I was only a few yards away from him watching his every move.

I sighed. It could all be quite innocent. A guy and his girlfriend who had had too much to drink maybe or that they were feeling romantic. That sort of thing.

But as I began cleaning up my room, I couldn't shake the thought of how the man kept looking around like you might expect someone who was up to no good would act. He definitely seemed like someone who was doing something he shouldn't have been doing. I had seen enough movies to recognize how a guilty person acted and that man, whoever he was, just didn't seem like he was on the level.

That night I dreamed about him. It was more like a nightmare. When I woke up in the morning, I could remember the dream just as though it was a movie. It was disturbing to say the least and I tried to dismiss it from my mind, but I wasn't having much success.

I rode down to the beach the next day on my bike. It was a Saturday so Mrs. Johnson wasn't there to bug me. And Mom never seemed to mind where I went as long as I was home in time for supper. I was wishing Mom would tell Mrs. Johnson that it was okay for me to be riding around on my own and that I didn't usually get into any trouble. I guess I was just going to have to have a talk with Mom and let her know how I felt about Mrs. Johnson's constant rein on my freedom.

When I got to the beach, it didn't feel like it usually did. It felt kind of scary. I couldn't help remembering the man who had carried the lady into the trees so close to my little fort that it gave me the willies. I didn't want to be there any more in case that man turned up again in his car. I hated the thought of having to give up my fort, but there was no way I was going to hang around there with the fear that the man would turn up again. What if the lady he was carrying wasn't sleeping at all. What if she was dead. That was a scary thought.

I put down my bike and walked along the treeline where I thought the man carrying the lady had entered. I didn't want to hang around any longer than necessary, but I was curious. What if there was some sign of a gravesite or something like that where that man had buried the woman? It was possible, but it didn't seem very probable to me. But I had to satisfy my curiosity.

I made a quick search amongst the trees, but I didn't see anything that looked suspicious. If the man had buried her nearby, surely there would have been a sign, like a mound or a hole maybe. But there was nothing as far as I could see. After a couple of minutes, I got out of there. It was too spooky for me. I didn't know what I would do if the guy turned up suddenly and saw me looking around in here. I would probably faint and then the guy would know for sure that I knew something that I shouldn't have known, seen something I shouldn't have seen.

I pedalled home as fast as I could, sure that the guy was following me in his car, maybe wanting to run over me. But nothing happened and I breathed a sigh of relief when I got home. I never wanted to go down there ever again, fort or no fort. I was just going to have to find a new place where I could enjoy my solitude.

CHAPTER TWO

I never did find another place where I could enjoy my solitude. I'm not sure why. Maybe it was because my original fort was such a perfect setup for me that I figured I could never find another spot like that again. Or maybe it was because the whole incident with that man carrying the woman into the trees had spooked me so much, the idea of being caught out there by myself didn't sit very well with me.

It took me a long time to forget about what I had seen that day. Actually, I still think about it sometimes. I haven't told anybody except my mom about how I feel and I hadn't been very honest with her. Maybe if I had shared my thoughts with somebody, I would have been able to forget all about it. After all, there was probably nothing to it. Nothing ever appeared in the paper about a woman disappearing so all that worry and thinking that somebody had been murdered practically on top of my little fort was all for nothing. Now that I'm fifteen, I have to chuckle at what a wimp I was way back then. Thinking about it now, I wonder what all the fuss was about and why I was so scared and had all those nightmares. What a waste. I mean, the guy wasn't even that scary looking. He was just an ordinary guy dressed up in a camouflage outfit. Nothing extraordinary about that. It's not as though he had evil-looking eyes or a moustache like Hitler or a pock-marked face.

One day shortly after my fifteenth birthday, Mom told me she wanted to have a talk to me. She looked really serious. Oh, oh, what had I done now that prompted this? I racked my brain trying to think about what I had done that Mom might have found not to her liking. My report card hadn't been great, but it wasn't that bad. As far as I knew, none of my teachers had phoned home complaining about me. And I had been keeping my room as clean as possible – well, not exactly clean, but I've seen worse. My friend Arnie's room was about the worst I had ever seen. Mom would have had a bird if my room looked anything like his.

"I know it's been hard on you not having a dad," Mom said, once we had settled in the living room and my sisters were over at my grandma's. "It must be hard not having somebody to talk to about things that are on your mind. You know, man things that you wouldn't want to talk to me about." She looked really serious and I couldn't help wondering what was coming next. Was she getting married? No, that didn't seem likely. There hadn't been any men around and Mom rarely went out at night, so it couldn't be that. Besides, my dad had never contacted us, so Mom was still married. She couldn't exactly get married again even if she wanted to. That would be like committing polygamy.

"Since you don't have a dad, I've decided to enter you into a program called Big Brothers," Mom continued. "Maybe you've heard about it." When I shook my head, Mom continued. "Men volunteer to become like mentors to young boys to help them sort through things that might confuse them about life. It's a great program and I thought it would be a wonderful opportunity for you to be able to talk over things with an adult." She paused, looking at me expectantly. "What do you think, Ryan?"

I shrugged, somewhat relieved that Mom hadn't wanted to talk about something I had done that she didn't approve of. It was one of the nicest things about my mom that I could think of. She wasn't into blaming or finding fault or grounding me for bad behavior all the time. She was very accepting and even overlooked some of the things that I had done that I wasn't exactly proud of, like being caught raiding the neighbor's cherry trees and gorging on cherries until I got sick.

"I...I don't know," I told her. "I guess it would be okay, depending on whether I liked the guy. Who is he?"

"Well, I haven't got that far yet. I thought I would talk it over with you before I actually signed you up for the program. If it sounds like something you wouldn't want to do, I definitely wouldn't push you into it. I just thought it would be a wonderful opportunity for you."

I knew Mom wanted me to tell her that I thought it was a great idea and that I was really keen, but I really wasn't. As far as I was concerned, everything seemed to be going along pretty good in my life so why did I need some stranger to come meddling in it? I was keeping out of trouble and my world seemed much to my liking as it was. The only exception was my two sisters. They were just as objectionable as they had always been. Thank heavens they only fought between themselves and rarely involved me, but it got pretty exasperating having to listen to them day and night arguing about just about anything. Those two had never agreed on one thing since they were born.

"I...I guess it would be okay." I didn't want to give her a ringing endorsement. Maybe if she thought I was just lukewarm on the subject, she would forget about the whole thing. Then I wouldn't have to feel guilty about not wanting to do it and ruining her plan to provide me with a substitute father.

"Well. That's wonderful." She gave me one of her winning smiles and reached over and gave me a big hug. "I think you're doing the right thing, dear. I'm sure you won't regret it. I'll let them know right away that you are a candidate."

I sighed. My plan to not seem enthusiastic hadn't worked at all. In fact, Mom seemed to think that I was really keen. Wow, had I ever misjudged that scenario. I smiled weakly over at her, trying to put on the best face possible, resigned to my fate. My only hope now was that they wouldn't be able to find anybody suitable.

After all, it was a volunteer thing according to Mom. Surely there weren't that many men out there who wanted to spend several hours a week talking to a teenager. I couldn't imagine anything worse if I was an adult.

"Do you think Dad will ever come back home?" I suddenly asked her. We hadn't talked much about Dad's disappearance. I hadn't wanted to bring up the topic because I knew how hurt she was that Dad had just left without even so much as a note to tell us where he was going and why. Now, four years later and we hadn't heard a word from him, the thought that maybe he would return some time still lingered.

"I don't know, Ryan. But I wouldn't get my hopes up if I were you. He's been gone a long time."

"How would you feel if he did come back?" I really wanted to know whether Mom had given up on him completely or whether she still hoped he might return. And if he did, would that make her happy or would she tell him to get lost.

"I really don't know. This is still his home technically, but would I welcome him? I'm not sure. I guess it would depend on whether he had changed and why he left in the first place. We've done very well without him. I know you miss not having a dad and that's one of the reasons I contacted the Big Brothers Organization—so that you would have a father substitute to talk to."

"He wasn't much of a dad when he was here," I told her. "He didn't talk to me much, we didn't do anything together."

"Well, that won't be the case if you have a Big Brother. They will take you places and give you the opportunity to talk about things that are bothering you." She smiled at me. "You're going to really like the program. I'm very excited about it."

After several weeks had passed, I was totally convinced that nothing was going to happen and that Mom had given up hope and I could continue my carefree ways without having to put up with some stranger butting into my business. Unfortunately, Mom hadn't given up hope and a couple of days after I was beginning to celebrate, she informed me that the Big Brothers foundation had found a match and that I would be meeting him within the next few days. I felt ill. Maybe I should just declare my displeasure to Mom and bring this whole thing to an end. After all, it was my life wasn't it? Surely, I had some say in what I preferred even though I was only fifteen. But again, my conscience began to bother me. I hated disappointing my mom. She was such a great mom and always treated me like an adult, always considering my feelings. It would be a kind of sacrilege to suddenly tell the truth about how I felt. I just couldn't do it.

When the time came to meet my so-called mentor, my Mom was so excited, I had to laugh. It was almost like she was about to go on a date or something. She was quite giggly and kept assuring me that this was going to be a turning point in my life. I wasn't quite sure what she meant by that. As far as I was concerned, my life was going along pretty well. I didn't consider myself a typical snotty-nosed teenager who was constantly looking for trouble with a loathing for all adults. That just wasn't me. Any psychiatrist would have given me an A plus as far as being well adjusted. I was certain of that. Well, fairly certain. I wasn't perfect. After all, I was fifteen. What could one expect?

"Your Big Brother will be coming in a couple of minutes," Mom said, glancing at her watch. "This is so exciting. Aren't you excited, Ryan?"

"Oh…sure. It'll be great." I almost choked on the words. I felt like a hypocrite. But I was determined to grin and bear it. Who knew, maybe it wasn't going to be all that awful. Maybe the guy would be a really nice person. Stranger things had happened.

When the knock on the door finally came, Mom rushed to answer it. I was in my room trying to make myself busy, hoping against hope that maybe the guy had gotten a flat tire or had an accident and wouldn't be coming, but no such luck. I could hear Mom welcoming him, her voice a couple of octaves louder than usual. I could just see her in my mind's eye fluttering around making the guy feel comfortable, probably offering him a cup of coffee. If there was one thing my mom was the world's best at, it was being sociable and making people feel relaxed.

"Ryan," she called, after several minutes, "Mr. Swenson is here. Come and meet him."

I took a deep breath and ambled toward my bedroom door, prepared for the worst. When I entered the living room, I got the shock of my life. Mr. Swenson was sitting on the couch across from my mom. He stood up and walked toward me with his hand out.

"Nice to meet you, Ryan. A real pleasure. You can call me Joe."

I was frozen to the spot, unable to move, shocked beyond belief. Was I going to faint?

"Shake hands with Mr. Swenson, Ryan," Mom said, when she noticed that I was just standing there looking stunned.

The reason I was looking stunned was because Mr. Swenson looked just like the man I had seen at the beach carrying the woman into the trees. He wasn't dressed in a camouflage outfit, but I was convinced it was the same man. He still had his hand out and he was still smiling, but I seemed totally unable to move, even when Mom insisted that I shake hands with the man.

Mr. Swenson chuckled. "Well, young man, I know how it is meeting somebody new, somebody you don't know anything about. Now don't you worry about shaking hands with me if you don't want to. There's nothing to say that you have to do that. I'm sure we'll soon get to know each other and that's what matters the most."

"Ryan, what has come over you?" Mom said. She turned to Mr. Swenson, who had returned to the couch and continued to smile as though nothing out of the ordinary had occurred.

"You'll have to excuse my son for his bad behavior. He isn't usually like this. He is usually very polite."

I was wishing the floor under me would open up and I could just disappear forever. I took a deep breath and looked over at my mom. She looked really hurt and confused by the way I was acting. I had to do something to rescue the situation, but my body and my mind weren't cooperating. Finally, I stumbled over and sat down beside her.

"If you would rather that I come at another time," Mr. Swenson said. "That would be okay with me. I know these things can be quite overwhelming for a young person."

Mom looked at me. "Would you prefer to do this at another time, Ryan?"

I shook my head, afraid to look at Mr. Swenson for fear I might freeze up again. "It's okay," I managed. I knew it wasn't okay, but what else could I say? I couldn't exactly tell her that this guy was the guy from the beach, that he might be a…killer or a kidnapper or something worse.

Mom didn't look very convinced. She reached over and put her arms around me. "You've got me really worried, Ryan. I wish I knew what was bothering you. This just isn't like you to act this way."

"I'm sorry, Mom. I'll be all right. I guess I just panicked a little bit." I glanced over at Mr. Swenson, who was still smiling and seemed totally unaffected by my bad behavior. I would have thought by this time that he would have been out the door never to return.

"Well, if you're sure," Mom said. She looked at me for a long time as though waiting for me to tell her that I wanted to call the whole thing off. When I didn't say anything, she smiled over at Mr. Swenson. "Today was just going to be about you two getting to know one another. We certainly appreciate you volunteering to spend time with Ryan and answer questions he might have about…you know…life and problems he might have at school and that sort of thing."

"I'm certainly willing to do that and more," Mr. Swenson said. "Before we get started, I would like to know about what kinds of things you are interested in, Ryan, what hobbies you have, what you think about the world and what you would like to do for your life's work. That kind of thing. I would also like us to go places that interest you, maybe to the museum or the zoo or hiking or just hanging out in the park throwing a frisbee around."

"Ryan likes to ride his bike and go down to the beach. He used to go there quite a bit, but lately—"

"Mom," I interrupted. "I don't go down there anymore." That was all I needed, to let Mr. Swenson know that I hung out at the very place he— I couldn't even finish the thought. I looked over at him, but his expression hadn't changed. He was either a very good actor or was it possible that I was getting all in a flurry over nothing? Maybe this man wasn't the same man even though he looked exactly like the person I had seen that day. And even if he was the same man, maybe what he had done could have been perfectly innocent. My mind was a jumble of conflicting thoughts. How was I going to go through with this charade, pretending to be a fifteen-year-old anxious to hear the wisdom from an older man when that man might be—what? Either totally innocent or at the worst a killer.

"I've got a bike myself," Joe said. "Maybe we could go cycling around town, looking at the sites, maybe do a little exploring. What do you think?"

He looked over at me expectantly. I looked at Mom, who was smiling now, obviously happy that I was beginning to cooperate. "I guess that would be okay." Somehow, I couldn't imagine myself pedalling down the street with this guy knowing what I knew about him. Besides, I enjoyed riding around on my bike by myself. I didn't need company. I didn't want any company and I certainly didn't want somebody asking me a bunch of stupid questions about whether I liked school or if I had a girlfriend or whether I had thought about what I wanted to do as my life's work.

"That's wonderful," Mom said. "I'm going to go into the kitchen and finish cleaning up in there and let you two get to know one another. I can't thank you enough for what you are doing, Mr. Swenson. And I'm sure Ryan appreciates it too."

"Call me Joe," he said. "You make me feel like an old man when you call me Mr. Swenson." He laughed. "My students call me Mr. Swenson, but you guys can call me Joe. Keeps it less formal don't you think?"

"Well, Joe, I hope you and Ryan have a nice talk." Mom started toward the kitchen and then stopped. "Are you sure you won't have a coffee or something?"

"I'm just fine, Mrs. Sinclair. Just fine."

Mom chuckled. "Now you call me Marjorie or I'm just going to have to start calling you Mr. Swenson again."

Once Mom was out of the room, I suddenly felt panicky. What was I supposed to say to this man? I couldn't think of a single thing I wanted to talk to him about. Maybe I should ask him what he did to that woman he had carried into the trees. That would shake him up. Maybe he would be out the door never to return. But I couldn't do that. For one thing it would be rude and for another maybe I had been wrong about him. After all, it was possible this wasn't the same man, wasn't it? After all, it was three years ago and I hadn't really got a good look at him.

"I can see you're not as keen about doing this as your mom," Joe said, looking over at me, rubbing his chin and looking thoughtful. "I guess I can't blame you there, me being a stranger and all. But I'm not such a bad guy. I think if you give us a chance, we'll get along just fine."

I wanted to laugh at that. *If I gave it a chance?* What a joke. I wanted to give it a chance like I wanted to jump off the Powell Street Bridge.

"So, what do you think, Ryan?" he asked, when I hadn't replied. "Are you willing to give it a try?"

I wanted to say no in the worst way, but I didn't want to disappoint Mom. After all, she had gone to a lot of trouble to set all this up for me despite the fact that I didn't appreciate it in the least. Finally, I nodded. "I guess it would be okay," I managed.

He laughed. "This isn't going to be like a visit to the dentist. I'll do my best to make it fun for you."

"I'll be okay," I added. "I just have to get used to it I guess."

Later, as I sat at on my bed looking out the window and thinking about my talk with Mr. Swenson, I wondered how I was ever going to go through with this. I wasn't very good at pretending and it looked as though I was going to have to do a lot of that. And what if he started asking me a lot of questions about my spending time at the beach? I wished Mom hadn't mentioned that little fact. Mr. Swenson might put two and two together and figure I might have seen something that could land him in jail. That is if he really was the man I was afraid he was. I hoped that he wasn't, but the more I looked at him, the surer I became. That bushy hair and the moustache convinced me.

"Well, how did it go?" Mom wanted to know once Mr. Swenson was out the door. "Did you like him? I thought he was a really nice man."

I shrugged. "He was okay I guess."

"Ryan, I don't understand. Why are you so reluctant to do this? I thought you would be really happy to have somebody to talk things over with since your dad is obviously never coming back. It's a wonderful opportunity for you."

"I'm sorry, Mom. I'll really try to like him. I know how much it means to you."

Mom laughed. "Ryan, I'm not the one who has to like him. You're the one who will be spending time with the man. If you don't want to do this, you just have to say so and I'll cancel the whole thing." She looked over at me with that look on her face that told me how disappointed she would be if I told her to forget about it, that I never wanted to see the guy again. "The girls sure liked him. They thought he was very handsome."

"They must be blind," I said. "Or just plain stupid. Oh yeah, they're my sisters. That explains everything." Why didn't I just explain everything to Mom. How I suspected that Mr. Swenson was the guy I saw at the beach, the guy carrying the unconscious woman into the tree? But I just couldn't seem to bring myself to do it. I could be wrong and that would be worse than having to put up with a few visits with the man. Maybe with any luck, he would get tired of my lack of enthusiasm and give up on me.

"Your sisters aren't stupid, Ryan." She stood, hands on hips looking at me as though seeing me for the first time. "You don't seem to be yourself today. Is something bothering you?"

There was plenty bothering me, but I wasn't about to tell my mom that. "Everything's just ducky," I told her, giving her my most ingratiating smile. She didn't look convinced but shrugged and went back into the kitchen.

My life was becoming more complicated by the minute.

CHAPTER THREE

For the next three days I couldn't seem to think about anything but having to spend my valuable time with Mr. Joe Swenson Esquire, a man I was certain had a shady past. In fact, I had been a witness to some of that shadiness and was wishing that I could just disappear off the surface of the earth in order to avoid him. But that wasn't going to happen. Maybe it wasn't too late to call the whole thing off. Yes, that was the perfect solution. Mom would be disappointed, really put out, but at least I would be spared all this agony of having to play a role that I knew I wasn't in the least capable of pulling off. I rolled my eyes, looked up at the ceiling and knew that wasn't going to happen. Who was I kidding? My fate was already sealed and nothing short of a hurricane or World War 111 was going to change it.

When the day finally arrived that I was to have my first outing with Joe (why was I calling him Joe? Joe seemed like a name for a buddy and Mr. Swenson was exactly the opposite to that) I sat in my room counting the seconds when the front doorbell would ring and Joe would appear smiling and eager to begin our fantastic adventure together.

As I watched the hands of the clock reach the designated hour and Joe still hadn't arrived, my heart began to beat with the excitement that he had either forgotten about me, got into an accident, or decided that maybe being a Big Brother wasn't something he wanted to do after all. Maybe the gods were on my side and had decided to spare me. As far as I was concerned, I certainly deserved their sympathy.

Those thoughts were abruptly put to rest when, at three minutes after his designated time of arrival, the doorbell rang. It sounded like my death knoll.

"Ryan," my mom yelled at me from somewhere down the hallway. "That's probably Mr. Swenson at the door. Please answer it. I'm busy helping the girls."

I left my bedroom and sauntered toward the door. When I opened it, there he was and he was still smiling. Didn't he have any other expression? Was his face permanently frozen into a goofy grin that was obviously meant to soften me up and make me feel all gooey inside with the anticipation of hearing his words of wisdom?

"Well, hello again, Ryan. Nice to see you. How's everything going?"

"Fine," I said, stepping aside and allowing him to enter. Mom and my two sisters came into the room, obviously awed by our visitor as they stood admiring him.

"Welcome, Joe," my mom said. "Please, have a seat, make yourself comfortable." She gestured toward the couch. "Can I get you anything?"

"I'm fine," Joe said, sitting down and looking over at me. "What do you think, Ryan? Are you raring to go?"

"Yeah, sure," I managed. I wasn't raring to go, but I didn't want to be rude with Mom sitting there looking expectant and my sisters staring at me enviously.

"Any idea where you're going?" my mom asked, settling on the edge of the couch. My two sisters stood google-eyed the whole time. You would think they had never seen a full-grown man before.

"I thought maybe we'd go down to the beach. I've got my bike in the back of my truck. Are you up to that, Ryan? I know you like riding your bike and the beach is just a nice little jaunt from here."

Horror of horrors. That was the last place I wanted to go. Why had he picked the beach when there were so many other places to explore? Then I remembered Mom telling him how much I liked going to the beach. Why had I opened my big mouth?

"I used to go there a lot, myself," Joe continued. "It was one of my favorite places, but I haven't been there in a long time. It'll be nice to visit again, see how it's changed over the years."

The way he was looking at me, I was convinced he could read my mind and knew that I had seen him with that poor lady. Now I really felt panicky. How was I going to go through with this? Maybe he had something in mind for me, like an accident or something. Was I about to go on my last bike ride? Maybe he had drowning on his mind or suffocation or a bike accident that would maim me for life, cause me to be in a permanent coma.

"Ryan would really like that," my mom said. "He used to go down there a lot. In fact, I think he had a little hideout there that he liked to spend time in. Ryan has always been a little bit of a lone wolf. He doesn't have a lot of friends." She looked over at me and smiled. "That's why I thought spending some time with an adult might be good for him, help him come out of himself and gain some confidence, if you know what I mean. Not having a dad has been especially hard on him." My sisters chuckled. I wasn't sure what they found so amusing considering that they might never see me again. I glared at them, but that seemed to just make them act sillier.

Joe stood up, smiled at the girls which caused them to giggle even more and then turned to me. "Well, chum, what do you think? Should we be off on our venture into the unknown?"

I was barely able to nod my head, desperately trying to pull myself together. Being called "Chum" didn't exactly please me either. What was the matter with him? Had he forgotten my name

23

already? "Chum?" What a ghastly name to call anybody. Maybe a dog would appreciate it, but I certainly didn't.

I watched him get his bike out of the back of his car while the girls and Mom watched from the front step. It looked like a pretty fancy mountain bike that probably cost thousands of dollars compared to mine that Mom had gotten for me at Walmart.

"Here we go," he said, waving to Mom and the girls. You would have thought we were going on a fifty- mile marathon or something, the way they were acting. Well, maybe they would be sorry if they never saw me again.

I followed Joe as we wended our way through the downtown area and finally ended up on the road that led to the beach. I was wishing Mom hadn't said anything about my fort. That was likely to alert Joe to the fact that maybe I had been hidden there at the very time that he had carried that lady into the trees and done who knew what to her.

As luck would have it, he rode right near where my fort had been and stopped, looking toward the trees and then over at me. "Is your little hideout anywhere near here?" he asked, giving me a look that made my skin crawl. It was the first time he wasn't smiling. It was almost as though he had turned into another person.

"No," I said. "It's further on, around the corner, but it's probably not much to look at now after so many years." I smiled at him, feeling suddenly that maybe I could fool him into thinking that I was just a stupid kid and hadn't seen anything, that I didn't suspect him of being a criminal.

He laid his bike down on the sand and sat down, gesturing for me to do the same. We sat looking out over the water for several minutes, a gentle breeze coming off the water, keeping it from being too hot.

"Nice place, isn't it?" he finally said, not looking at me. "I bet you came down here a lot."

I shrugged. "Not really. Maybe once or twice a week." I wondered when he was going to make his move. Surely, he suspected that I knew something, that I had seen something that day almost three years ago. What did he plan to do to me? What could he do to me with people not far away from us enjoying the beach? It might be hard for him to start chocking me without being seen by someone.

I was wishing I could be anywhere except where I was at that precise moment. Joe kept looking over at me as though trying to make up his mind whether I had seen something I shouldn't have seen or not. I smiled at him doing my best to look as innocent as possible. I wasn't ready to die at the age of fifteen, especially at the hands of this man whom I was beginning to really despise.

"So, tell me, Ryan, what you really like doing in your spare time. You must have some hobbies or something that really turns your crank."

His question surprised me. What did he care what my interests were? His real motive for coming down here was surely to find out what I had seen that day. This whole Big Brother thing was just a cover-up.

"I don't have any hobbies. I like reading and riding my bike. That's about it."

"What kind of books do you like to read?"

I shrugged. "I don't know. Just any kind that interest me. Mom brings some home from the library for me and my sisters. They don't like to read much. They're too busy arguing with each other to bother with books."

"I've got lots of books at my place. I'll bring some over next time I come. You might like some of them."

I was sure I wouldn't like them and I was hoping that maybe we wouldn't be meeting again, but that hope didn't seem likely if my mom had anything to say about it.

"I lost my dad a few years ago," he continued. "So, I know how you must feel not having a dad. I was pretty upset. My dad and I were very close, we did a lot of things together so it left a pretty big hole in my life."

"My dad and me didn't do anything together. I don't think he even liked me."

"What makes you say that?"

I glanced at him. He was staring at me as though he really wanted to know. I found that strange considering the kind of a person he probably was. I didn't want to discuss my thoughts with this man, but if I was going to convince him that I hadn't seen him doing anything, I would have to play along with him, string him along. "He ignored me most of the time and the only time he spoke to me was when he caught me doing something I shouldn't have been doing. We never went anywhere together. He never took me to any ball games or movies. The only thing he seemed to be interested in was drinking beer."

I could hardly believe I was opening up to this guy. Why was I doing that? What a waste of time.

"I'm sorry to hear that," he finally said, looking at me as though he really meant it. I knew he didn't. I knew he was just playing me for a sucker and that my little problems were the least of his worries.

We sat for a long time without saying anything, looking out at the water, enjoying the breeze that wafted into our faces. There weren't many people at the beach at this time of day. There was a couple with their dog, throwing a frisbee around and another couple lying under an umbrella.

"I always liked the beach when I was younger," Joe said. "My friends and I used to come down here and have wiener roasts and that kind of thing. We were a pretty wild bunch back then, but we had a lot of fun. We didn't get into too much trouble." He laughed. "What about you, Ryan? What do you and your friends like to do?"

"I don't have many friends. I stick pretty much to myself. There's a guy in our neighborhood that I hang out with sometimes, but he's kind of crazy. Sometimes we raid fruit trees together and bug the neighbors by knocking on their doors and hiding across the street." I looked over at Joe and shrugged. "Guess I shouldn't be doing that, but it fills the time anyway. It's better than sitting in my room listening to my sisters arguing."

Joe laughed. "If that's the worst thing you do, I don't think you got much to worry about."

I was surprised that Joe didn't make any mention of my fort or say anything about what might have taken place here three years ago. I was also surprised that he seemed so friendly considering that he probably knew that I had the goods on him. I was relieved that he hadn't tried to hurt me in any way. Maybe he intended to wait for a more opportune time. After all, assaulting a kid at the beach with people around wouldn't exactly have been very smart on his part.

By the time we got back to our place, it was getting toward suppertime. I was relieved to get back home in one piece and not have to worry about anybody hurting me, namely Joe Swenson. I knew he could easily have forced me to cough up what I knew about what he had done simply by twisting my arm behind my back until I couldn't stand it, but he hadn't done that.

"Well, how did you two make out?" Mom wanted to know, when we entered the house. "Did you have fun at the beach?"

I wouldn't have exactly called it having fun, but then again it hadn't been all that bad. Considering what Joe was hiding and the kind of person he was, as far as I was concerned, I had dodged a bullet. If I didn't know what he was guilty of, I would have probably enjoyed our time together, but I knew he was just playing along with me, waiting for an opportune time to force me to cough up the truth.

"We had a really nice visit," Joe said. "There weren't many people at the beach, so we kind of had it to ourselves. It gave us some time to talk about a few things."

Mom beamed, looking at me as though I had just won a medal or something. "I'm so glad. I was a little worried that Ryan was going to be…well, not enthusiastic considering how he was the last time we spoke." She laughed. "I guess it was just a matter of breaking the ice and Ryan getting used to talking to an adult besides his mom."

"He was just fine," Joe said. "No problem. It was a real pleasure spending some time with him. He's a great kid."

Boy, he was really laying it on thick, I thought. I wasn't a great kid for one thing and for another, he was just setting me up for another visit. I was a real threat to him and he knew it.

The girls came running into the room, not wanting to miss the opportunity to see Joe again and curious about my visit with him.

"Hi girls," Joe said. "You've got a real nice brother here. Did you know that?"

My sisters looked at one another and then over at me, their expressions and the rolling of their eyes revealing what they thought about that declaration.

"He's a brat," Angela said. "And he's always trying to tell us what to do."

My mom glared at the girls. "Now that isn't nice, Angela. Remember, you've only got one brother."

"That's one too many," Sara said.

Joe laughed. "You two girls remind me of my sisters. They weren't entirely enthusiastic about me either, but now that we're adults, I think they appreciate me a little more."

That night I sat in my room thinking about my time with Joe at the beach. As much as I hated to admit it, he really seemed like a nice guy. If I didn't know what I knew about him and that girl he had carried into the trees, I would have thought he was quite a decent person. I was beginning to wish that I had never seen what had taken place that day. If I hadn't, maybe I would be looking forward to seeing Joe again and eager to listen to what he might have to say to me about things. I felt caught between my mom wanting Joe and I to somehow bond like a father and son and at the same time not wanting to have anything to do with him at all. In fact, I would have liked to go down to the police station and report him, but something kept me from doing that. Maybe it was because I wasn't totally sure that Joe was the guy I had seen that day. He looked just like him, but what if I was wrong? That would be awful – to accuse somebody of something like that and then discover that it wasn't true at all. The very thought gave me the shivers. What would my mom think of me, let alone Joe himself and the cops? They would think I was just a troublemaker of some kind.

I tried not to think about Joe Swenson over the next few weeks, but despite not wanting to think about what he had done, my mind kept going back to that day when I had clearly seen him carrying that lady into the trees. At the time I had thought maybe the lady was just asleep, but the more I thought about it, the more I convinced myself that she wasn't asleep at all. I was almost sure that she was dead, just by the way he was carrying her and by the way he kept looking around as though checking to see if anybody was watching him. If there was anybody who looked guilty, it was him.

Joe was due to pay me another visit soon, a visit I wasn't looking forward to any more than the previous visit. I was sure he wasn't looking forward to it any more than I was, but he had to find out what I knew one way or another and also whether I had gone to the cops. It gave me a strange feeling knowing that I held Joe Swenson's future in my hands. It wasn't something I relished, but I felt an obligation to do what was right. What my next move was going to be I had no idea. Should I just play along and act innocent hoping that Joe would eventually be convinced that I didn't know anything, or should I go to the cops and tell them everything I knew?

I pondered the latter solution for several days and had all but convinced myself that the police would never take me seriously. A fifteen-year-old with a story about some guy carrying a woman into the bushes that he had witnessed three years ago? They would probably think I was either hallucinating or having nightmares and have a good laugh at my expense after sending me home promising to look into it. Not the most promising outlook as far as I was concerned.

I knew I couldn't talk over my suspicions with Mom. She already thought Joe was just about the most wonderful human being ever to grace the earth and couldn't stop talking about him and how lucky I was to have somebody like him to spend time with. I could just see her expression when I told her what I had seen at the beach. "And you think that was Mr. Swenson?" she would ask looking at me as though I was insane. "Mr. Swenson is the kindest, nicest man I know. He wouldn't hurt a flea. You must be mistaken. After all, that happened three years ago when you were only twelve. You can't possibly be certain that the man you saw was Mr. Swenson. It could have been anybody."

Then what would I say? That I was sure it was him, as sure as I was standing there. I couldn't say that because I wasn't one hundred percent certain in my own mind. Maybe I was ninety percent certain, but that little bit of uncertainty would be enough to convince my mom that I was dead wrong.

I decided that Arnie was the only person I could talk this over with. Not that Arnie would magically come up with a solution, but because I had a sense that he could keep a secret and that maybe he could help me make a decision about my next move.

I told him at lunch hour in the cafeteria that I wanted to talk to him about something. He looked a little surprised. We hung out together quite a lot. He only lived about six blocks away and I had known him since Kindergarten. I liked him a lot, maybe because he was a lot more confident than I was and didn't mind saying outrageous things. He wasn't one of the in crowd and kept to himself pretty much.

"What do you want to talk to me about?" he asked, looking at me as though I was planning to coerce him into joining a gang about to pull off a heist. I had to laugh at his expression. Arnie is a very thoughtful guy and probably the last guy on earth to ever do anything underhanded. He was about as honest as anybody I had ever known. A little skeptical maybe, but essentially a nice guy. What I liked most about him was that he didn't care at all about being popular or about what other people thought of him. He was his own man and the rest of the world could go jump in the lake as far as he was concerned. He also had a droll sense of humor that amused me to no end.

"I got a problem," I told him. "I need a little advice."

"I don't come cheap," he said, grinning broadly. "And I don't dole out advice to just anybody."

"Not even to your best friend?" I tried to look hurt.

He laughed. "I haven't got any friends and that includes my parents." When I gave him a solemn look, he took pity on me. "Well, maybe I could make an exception, but only this once."

"It involves a possible murder," I told him.

"Murder? Well, that is going to cost you plenty. It's not every day that I have to advise somebody about a murder case. Just where and when did this murder take place? And are you the murderer?"

"No, not me but my Big Brother."

"I didn't know you had a brother," Arnie said, looking askance. "I thought you only had those two little brats of sisters of yours."

"Not a real brother. You know, The Big Brothers. Older guys who volunteer to spend time with chumps like me, giving out advice and all that."

"I see," Arnold said, looking a little confused. "So why don't you ask him for advice? Surely that's what he's being paid for."

"He's not being paid at all. He's a volunteer. He does it out of the goodness of his heart. And I wouldn't ask him for advice because he's…he's the guy, the killer. I think he killed a woman."

That got Arnie's attention. "You're having me on, aren't you? Either that or you've been watching too many cop shows on television."

"I never watch television, and if I did, I wouldn't be watching cop shows."

"Why not? All that drama. It's the stuff of life. You could learn a lot watching cop shows."

I heaved a sigh. I didn't seem to be getting anywhere with Arnie. "Getting back to my original proposition." When I was certain I had his undivided attention, I told him everything: what I had seen and what I was now facing having to see Joe Swenson every couple of weeks. "It's really freaky, having to spend time with a killer or at least a suspected killer. I mean, I could be wrong. That's the worst part of this whole thing. I could be wrong. Maybe he's somebody who just looks a lot like the guy I saw that day."

Arnie gave me this kind of half smile. "You do know that eyewitness accounts are the least convincing evidence in a trial. Very unreliable." When I shook my head, he continued. "Anyway, that being said, here's my advice." He leaned in close to me and glanced around as though making sure nobody was listening. "Forget about it. Don't even think about what you saw. You were only twelve then, just a little kid. You can't tell me you remember that vividly after three years. God, I can't even remember what I was doing two days ago. Besides, at twelve years old, all adults look the same. You probably got all wound up and let your imagination run away with you. If I were you, I would just go along with this Big Brother of yours and treat him just like you would any other adult. The chances that this is the same guy you saw are pretty slim – like less than zero. Know what I mean?"

I sat looking at Arnie for several minutes, wanting to believe he was probably right but having a hard time of it. Murder was such a serious issue, it wouldn't be easy for me to just let it go on the off chance that Joe was completely innocent. Surely, I had an obligation to let the cops know what I had seen. Besides, this whole thing was going to bug me forever unless I took action. I had to be certain in my own mind that what I had witnessed was either completely innocent or that the man was not Joe Swenson.

"So how much do I owe you for that piece of valuable advice?" I asked, suddenly wanting to lighten the mood. Thinking about this whole thing day after day was beginning to get me down. I was desperate for a little bit of sunshine in my otherwise joyless life of late.

"You just happen to catch me in a charitable mood today my friend. You're off the hook. It's on the house." He gave me this goofy grin as though everything was right with the world and he had freed me of my little problem with his wise words. Unfortunately, I didn't feel any better than when I had sat down across from him. I sensed he was probably right, but what if he wasn't?

"Don't tell anybody about what we talked about," I said. "I wouldn't want it to get back to Joe. You know, just in case he really is innocent. Also, because if he knew what I suspected him of and he wasn't innocent, he might do something violent, if you know what I mean."

"You really are caught up in all this, aren't you? Lighten up old chap. It isn't the end of the world. The sun will rise tomorrow just as it always has and you will still be Ryan Sinclair, fifteen-year-old son of Mrs. Marjorie Sinclair."

"Thanks for that," I said. "I can now go home free in the knowledge that everything is right with the world. Ha!"

"If it would make you feel any better, you could go back to that little hideaway you had at the beach and do a thorough search. I mean, if the guy actually killed that woman he was carrying, he must have intended to bury her there somewhere. If you don't find anything, maybe that would make you feel a little better about things." Arnie grinned. "I won't charge you for that bit of advice either. My generosity knows no bounds today."

I took Arnie's advice and rode my bike down to the beach again with the vague hope of maybe finding something incriminating. I was somewhat reluctant three years ago, but now that I was older, the thought of finding a grave wasn't quite so intimidating.

After three years though, maybe finding some indication of where Joe had buried that woman would be wiped away completely. The thought of finding a dead body sent shivers up my back, however. I had never seen a dead body before and the thought of digging up a three- year- old corpse was even more frightening than I was prepared for.

By the time I got to where I thought Joe had entered the trees, I was beginning to have second thoughts. If I told anybody what I was doing, they would laugh and think I was just plain crazy and that my imagination was getting the better of me. But after some hesitation and making sure nobody was around, I entered the trees and began searching in earnest.

I didn't see any mounds or holes that would indicate that a body was buried there after searching for at least fifteen minutes. I wasn't sure what exactly to look for, but nothing stuck out. Was I on a fool's errand? Was Joe just what he seemed: a nice enough guy just doing what he thought as a responsible adult he should be doing: helping kids without fathers, giving them advice and maybe a shoulder to lean on?

I stood beside my bike looking out across the lake which on this particular afternoon was like a sheet of glass. My memory of Joe, if it was Joe, was still vivid in my mind. Seeing him carrying that poor woman limp in his arms wasn't something I was likely to ever forget. If I didn't get to the bottom of this, would I be haunted forever by this memory? I hoped not, because it was really bothering me and as far as I was concerned, no fifteen-year-old should have to carry around in their mind that kind of image.

That night I had a dream about Joe. In my dream, I asked him point-blank whether he had killed that lady and he just smiled, a really creepy smile, but he never answered me. I kept asking him, but I didn't get an answer no matter how many times I asked him. I was sure in my dream that he was guilty. Otherwise, why wouldn't he just say that he was innocent, that he hadn't killed anybody. When I woke up the next morning, I could remember the dream vividly just as though it had really happened. I couldn't help wondering what Joe's reaction would be if I actually asked him that question. I could never do that of course. What if he was guilty? What would he do to me? Maybe I would end up in some sandy grave of my own down at the beach.

As I lay thinking about my dream, I wondered if I should pose the question, just hypothetically, to my mom. What would her reaction be? Maybe she would take me seriously and actually offer a solution. The more I thought about it, the more I was certain that that was the way to go. I laughed to myself. Why hadn't I thought about this before? I decided that I would have to catch her in the right mood. Sometimes she was just too busy or preoccupied with something to bother about answering a hypothetical question.

In the following days, I kept watching my mom, waiting for the opportune moment, trying to discern when she was both in a good mood, which she almost was, and open to my somewhat macabre (I liked that word) question.

The opportunity came several nights later as we both sat watching a TV program. Whenever mom wanted to talk to me, she would mute the TV and ask me lots of questions about what I had done that day, how school was going and more serious questions like did I have any ideas about what I would like to do when I finished school? Did I want to go to college and if I did, what sorts of courses interested me.

After a lull in our conversation and just as mom was about to unmute the TV, I looked over at her and popped the question. "What would you do if you saw a murder or at least what looked like a murder, but you weren't sure. Maybe the person was asleep and not dead at all. Would you go to the police or just keep it to yourself?"

Mom gave me the most penetrating look. "Ryan, what kind of a question is that? Did this happen to you? Or is this something you've been reading in a detective novel?"

"No, I was just wondering, that's all."

"Ryan, you must have a reason for asking me something like that just out of the blue?" She was giving me that penetrating look again. "You've got me worried. What you've asked me is a very serious question. It's not something a fifteen-year-old should be thinking about. Or worried about for that matter, unless he actually witnessed what you've described. I want to know why you asked me that question, Ryan."

Now I had done it. Instead of getting an answer, I had upset my mom. How was I going to talk my way out of this one? I looked at her. Her brow was knitted in a strange pattern of concern. She looked ten years older than she had a few minutes earlier when we had just been sitting here watching TV. And I probably looked even guiltier than I felt. What in the world had possessed me to ask my mom a question like that? Was I entering early senility?

"Well?" she persisted. She wasn't going to let this go. She had me on a string and I suddenly knew what a fish must feel like when it's trying to wriggle off a hook.

I suddenly had an inspiration.

"It was a dream," I told her. "A very realistic dream. It really shook me up and I've been thinking about it every since."

It was clear by her expression that she didn't believe a word I was saying. She gave me that look. "Are you sure? You sounded pretty serious to me. Come on Ryan. This is your mother you're talking to. I didn't just crawl out from under a toadstool."

"Okay," I admitted. "It wasn't a dream. I actually saw a man carry a woman into the trees down at the beach when I was twelve. It's been bothering me ever since." I shrugged. "It's no big deal. He was probably trying to help her, don't you think?"

"I don't know, but it worries me that you have had that on your mind for three years. Why didn't you tell me before?"

Of course, I had told her, but she had obviously forgotten about it. Seeing Joe was what had triggered my memory and set me thinking that he had maybe murdered that lady. But I couldn't tell my mom that. She would definitely go off the deep end. The thought that she might be sending her boy off with a murderer would shake her up to no end.

"I don't know. I was just a little kid then. The thought that I could have been looking at a murder, didn't really hit me until I got a little older. By that time, I had kind of forgotten about it."

"Forgotten about it," Mom repeated, looking at me skeptically. "How could you forget about a murder? It must have scared you to death. And you've been carrying this around in your head for three whole years?" She sighed and put her arms around me. "You should have told me. I'm very disappointed. I'm your mother. I want you to feel that you can tell me anything, even if it's scary or worries you or you're concerned that I might disapprove."

"I thought maybe I was wrong about the whole thing. Maybe the man hadn't really murdered the lady. Maybe he was trying to help her. I was afraid of upsetting you. Sorry Mom."

We sat looking at one another for several seconds. I would have given anything to read her mind. I was surprised that she had forgotten that I had mentioned this three years ago. I guess it hadn't made much of an impression on her.

"Well," she finally said, "it was probably something perfectly innocent. I haven't heard anything about a murder at the beach or somebody missing in the last few years. I think it would be best to just try to put it out of your mind."

"I guess you're right," I told her, relieved that I had managed not to have to tell her that I thought the murderer was no other than my Big Brother, the man she had hand-picked to play the role of my substitute father.

CHAPTER FOUR

Joe Swenson appeared at our door two days later. I was laying on my bed listening to Bon Jovi on my earphones and hadn't heard the doorbell ring. When I came out of my room, there was my mom and Joe sitting together on the couch deep in conversation. Now what in the world could they be talking about? I wondered. They didn't even know each other very well, but by the way they were positioned on the couch, you would have thought they were best friends sharing long held secrets. I didn't like this scenario at all. I was hoping desperately, that she wasn't telling him about what I had seen down at the beach three years ago.

"Well, there you are," Mom said, giving me a surprising look. "I thought maybe you had gone out somewhere. Did you forget Joe was coming over today?"

"No, of course not, I just got carried away listening to—"

"Hey, Ryan," Joe said. "Nice to see you again."

"Joe and I were just talking and we've discovered that we went to the same school. What do you think of that?"

I didn't think much of it to tell you the truth. So what if they went to the same school. Lots of people in this town went to the same school. "Surprising," I said, not wanting to throw a damper on their obvious enthusiasm.

"Of course, Joe was a couple of years ahead of me," Mom continued, "but we had some of the same teachers and he knew some of the girls I chummed around with. Imagine that!"

I shrugged, not knowing how to react to Mom's wonderful news. She seemed very excited about it all, the most excited I had seen her in months.

I sat down across from them, looking down at my feet, wanting to shout that I didn't really care about whether they went to the same school. Big deal.

"So, are you all ready for another adventure?" Joe asked. "It's a great day out there."

"I guess so," I said.

"Well aren't we full of enthusiasm," Mom said. "Joe has sacrificed his time and put himself out for you and all you can say is 'I guess so'. Come on, Ryan. Buck up. This is a wonderful opportunity for you."

"It's not a big deal," Joe said, looking over at me with a grin. "Maybe you just don't feel like talking today. We can always do this another time if you'd rather."

"It's okay. I…don't mind…really."

"Ryan was telling me yesterday about something very traumatic that happened to him three years ago," Mom suddenly said. "Perhaps that's what's —"

"No, it isn't," I interrupted. "It has nothing to do with that. I'm fine, really. Joe and I will have a great time, Mom. You can bet on that." I was desperate to convince her and quickly that spending a couple of hours with Joe wasn't going to bother me. The alternative of her spilling the beans about me seeing a man carrying an unconscious woman into the trees was something I didn't want to tip Joe about. There was no telling what he would do to me if he thought I was a witness to his crime.

"Now that's more like it," Mom said, smiling over at me and looking relieved. "Maybe you could talk to Joe about what you told me yesterday, ask him what he thinks."

"No," I said. "I couldn't do that."

"And just why not?" Mom persisted. "After all, that's what Big Brothers are for. Right, Joe?"

"Right," Joe said. "Feel free to ask me anything. I'd be happy to help you work through whatever's bothering you."

"It's not bothering me." I tried to look unconcerned, but I don't think I was succeeding. They were both looking at me as though I was trying to hide something which is exactly what I was doing. Somehow, I had to change the subject and get them off my back. "So, where are we going today?" I asked Joe, giving him a grin that even the Cheshire Cat would have been proud of.

"We could go for a walk in the park," Joe said, "and then maybe stop at the Dairy Queen for a malt. How does that sound?"

"Sounds great to me," I said, looking at Mom and trying my best to look delighted. I didn't want her thinking that I didn't appreciate what Joe was doing for me. I hated upsetting my mom. She had enough on her mind just trying to referee my two sisters without me being a nuisance too.

There was a nice walk through the middle of the park that curved around and ended at the far end of the lake. It was quite spectacular, especially on a nice day, and attracted a lot of tourists, nature lovers and bird watchers. I would have much preferred riding my bike, but Joe seemed intent on walking so who was I to object? I guessed that he wanted to walk so he could quiz me on what my mom and I had talked about the day before, but I was definitely staying mum on that topic. I was thinking that he probably wanted to find out what I knew about what I had seen at the lake three years ago.

"Your mom seemed a little concerned," he said to me as we walked along. "Anything you want to talk to me about? I'm a pretty good listener."

I'll bet he was, I thought, especially since he was probably dying to know what this little kid saw and whether he would pose a threat.

"No. It's not really important," I told him. "Just something I saw a long time ago. I had practically forgotten about it. It's no big deal."

41

"It wouldn't hurt to talk about it," Joe persisted. "Sometimes it's good to talk things over that bother us."

I grinned over at him, trying my best to act as nonchalant as I could. "Well, you know how moms are. They exaggerate things all the time. Sometimes my mom gets real upset about nothing at all, blows it way out of proportion. I get a real kick out of it. I think she worries about me too much."

"Well, that's what mothers are for. Your mom's a real nice person. You're lucky to have a mom like her. Now if you ever met my mom, you would think yours was a real saint."

I looked up at him. "Oh yeah?" We had stopped beside a bench and Joe sat down. It looked as though he was settling in to have a long conversation with me, something I definitely wanted to avoid.

"Yeah, she wasn't really into parenting. We pretty much did what we wanted. My dad was on the road most of the time so he wasn't around much. It's a wonder I didn't end up in reform school or something."

Or maybe killing someone, I thought. I took a deep breath thankful that he couldn't read my mind. If he could, I would have been in real trouble.

We sat for a long time, watching the people in the park as they passed us, enjoying the perfect day and the pleasant surroundings. I had often ridden my bike through the park but had never thought that I would ever be there with somebody who had killed another human being. It gave me an eerie feeling. I wanted to run up to the first person I saw and tell them what I knew, shout it out to anybody who would listen, but I didn't. After all, there was the remotest chance that Joe wasn't guilty. Besides, I was beginning to like him a little bit despite what I knew about him. He didn't seem like a murderer, but mom always told me that what a person looked like on the outside was no indication of what they were like inside.

At the Dairy Queen, I guess Joe forgot all about quizzing me about what was bothering me and began asking me all kinds of goofy questions like did I have a girlfriend, what was my favorite subject at school, what kind of movies did I like and what did I want to be when I grew up. To be honest, I was relieved. Answering those kinds of questions was easy and seemed to satisfy Joe. I didn't have to lie or be evasive or anything like that.

After we finished having a malt, we walked back to my house. Mom was waiting anxiously and waved at us from the window as we approached. She was probably thinking that Joe and I had had a really serious discussion. I guess she was going to be pretty disappointed when I informed her that we hadn't talked about anything important at all.

"Well, you two, how was it? Did you have a good time? Did you enjoy the park? Did you see anybody you knew?"

I had to laugh at my mom. She was always so enthusiastic about everything, even a simple walk in the park. You would have thought we had gone on a trek across the world, the way she was smiling at us and giving me a hug. It was really nice to see her so happy. I was secretly very glad that she didn't know anything about Joe and what he had done. The fact that she remained ignorant of the kind of person he was, gave me a feeling of relief. I would hate to shatter her illusion of Joe, whom she really seemed to admire and like.

My sisters were almost as enthusiastic about Joe as my mom was, maybe even more enthusiastic. They always looked so google-eyed when he was around, you would have thought he was a movie star or something.

"We had a great time," Joe said, smiling over at my sisters as they stood looking at him. "Maybe you girls would like to come with us sometime. I'm sure Ryan wouldn't mind that."

He didn't have any clue how much I would mind that, I thought. They would drive him bonkers in no time and he probably would never come back. Then again, maybe that would be a good thing.

"Oh, could we?" Angela said to my mom. "That would be the greatest." Sara was jumping up and down as well.

My mom laughed, shaking her head and looking over at Joe who seemed to be enjoying the girls' enthusiasm. "I don't think so, girls. Mr. Swenson has enough on his plate helping your brother without two girls there to distract him. Right Joe?"

"Well, I don't know. It might be fun to have the girls come along once in a while. What do you think, Ryan?"

I glared over at my sisters. I think they knew the answer to that question before I even opened my mouth. "Definitely not a good idea," I said. "Isn't there a Big Sister's group in town?"

"I haven't heard of one," Mom said.

"I could look into it if you would like," Joe said.

My sisters didn't look happy. It was obvious they liked the idea of going on an outing with Joe. I think they saw him as a kind of romantic figure rather than a fatherly figure. They were getting to that age and I had to admit that Joe had the kind of good looks that a lot of young girls might find attractive even though he was old enough to be their father. He was more my mom's age.

That was when I looked over at my mom and suddenly had this horrible feeling. I definitely didn't like the way she was looking at Joe. It struck me as being a lot like the way my sisters were looking at him. Horror of horrors. Surely my mom had more sense than to see Joe as any kind of romantic figure. After all, she was married to my dad, wasn't she? Even though he hadn't shown his face around here for several years. This was all I needed----my mom falling for a murderer. I knew if that happened, I would have to spill the beans and tell her about my suspicions. And that was sure to open a whole new can of worms.

Suddenly, my life was becoming very complicated. What was I to do?

Later, as I sat in my room watching the fan go around and around, I tried to work things out in my mind. I couldn't let my mom walk into a situation where she could get hurt, maybe even murdered, just like that woman Joe had carried into the trees. I could never forgive myself if I kept my mouth shut and something bad happened to her. That would be the worst thing that could ever happen to anyone, let alone the fifteen-year-old son of a naïve mother.

I decided I would have to approach the topic cautiously without tipping her off as to what I was really wanting to know. I had to find out just how she felt about Joe and whether she would ever consider dating him. That could be tricky, but I was confident that I could pull it off without raising any alarms and getting my mom all hot and bothered. Mom wasn't born yesterday and usually tuned in pretty well when she thought I was being devious or asking her tricky questions. Whenever I lied to her, not that I did that very often and the lies I told were usually pale compared to some of the ones my sisters told, Mom was pretty good at reading me, so I was going to have to be particularly cautious.

That night, after my sisters had gone to bed (they always went an hour before me) and Mom and I were sitting in the living room together, I decided to put my little plan into action.

"So," I began, "what do you think of Joe, Mom? He seems like quite a nice guy, doesn't he?"

My mom was knitting me a sweater. She had knitted me quite a few of them, none of which I had worn much mainly because they were usually too big and baggy and the wool always made me itch.

"He's a very nice man," she said. "It's wonderful of him to spend his time helping young boys like you. I'm sure he has dozens of other things he would rather be doing."

"He's certainly very good looking. He must have a lot of girlfriends."

Mom laughed. "Now what would make you say a thing like that?"

"Oh, I don't know. My sisters sure seem to think he's really something."

Mom stopped knitting and looked over at me, giving me a puzzled look. "Is there something on your mind, Ryan? Is there something about Joe that is bothering you?"

"Ah…no, not really. I was just…making conversation. You know."

"No, I don't know. And you're making me very curious. Don't you like Joe? If you don't, I can always request somebody else. I would hate to do that, because you two seem to be getting along so well. And from my perspective, Joe seems like a wonderful man, a really fine person."

"So, you really like him?" I asked.

"Of course, who wouldn't?" She was looking at me in a curious way that made me squirm a little bit. I always felt like my mom could see right through me. Was I really that transparent?

"You're not jealous, are you?" she asked, picking up her knitting again and beginning to concentrate on that much to my relief. "If you are, I want you to know that you are the most important man in my life. Nobody could ever take your place. You're my heart and soul and you always will be."

I wasn't quite sure what to say after that. My mission to find out if Mom had any romantic intentions toward Joe hadn't gone quite the way I had hoped. In fact, it had gone quite counter to it. Now Mom was alerted to what might be going on in my head. If I was going to save her from falling for this guy, I wasn't doing a very good job.

Sure enough, about two weeks after Mom and I had had this little conversation, she took me aside and informed me that she and Joe were going out together. It wasn't actually a date, she explained. He had telephoned her and asked her if she would consider going out for a coffee. "Now I know we talked about this very thing," Mom said to me. "And I just want you to know that no matter what comes about, you are still my number one guy. I think Joe just wants to hook up with me and talk about how things are going between you two. I think it's a good idea."

It was a terrible idea as far as I was concerned. That he just wanted to talk about me was pure hogwash. Mom was still an attractive lady but she was still married to my dad, wasn't she? It was possible he could suddenly appear any day and then what would happen? Besides, Joe was a dangerous person. Hadn't I seen him drag that poor lady into the trees and bury her? No, I hadn't been able to find her grave, but that didn't mean she wasn't buried there. It was a large area and I wasn't entirely sure that where I had looked was the exact spot Joe had chosen to bury her.

What was I to do now? If I told Mom what I thought, she probably wouldn't believe me and would be very upset. Talk about sitting on a powder keg!

"I don't think it's a good idea at all," I said. "You don't know anything about him. He could be a …a criminal. Maybe he's been in jail or had done something against the law and the police just haven't clued into him."

Mom laughed. "Ryan, you can't possibly believe that. Joe wouldn't have been selected in the Big Brothers program if he had a record and had run afoul of the law in any way. They are very careful about who they choose to be mentors. Besides, you've spent some time with him. Does he seem like somebody that I should be wary of?"

"I don't know. Maybe. You told me once that appearances can be deceptive, that people aren't always what they appear to be." I felt proud of myself being able to use the very example she had used to back up my argument.

"Well, all things considered, I think I'll be quite safe in going out for a coffee with Joe."

I took a deep breath. I was determined to not let that happen. "He could be a sociopath or even worse, a pedophile. Did you notice the way he was looking at your daughters?"

"Ryan, whatever has come over you? Do you even know what a sociopath is or a pedophile? I can't believe you would think these things about Joe. You've got a some explaining to do, young man. Something is going on here and I want an explanation."

I hadn't seen my mom this mad for a long time, if ever. What had I done? She was glaring at me as though I was Darth Vader or somebody. "I'm sorry, Mom, I'm just trying to stop you from making a big mistake. Joe might seem like a great guy to most people, but to me he...well, I'm not so sure."

"And why is that? Do you know something I don't? You must have some reason for saying these things about him." She was standing now, hands on hips, her face red with anger. There was no way I was going to convince her not to keep that coffee date with Joe. She seemed to have already made up her mind. And in the meantime, she must think her only son has lost his mind completely.

"It's just a feeling I have," I continued, beginning to wish I hadn't gone all out on Joe like I had. After all, it was only a coffee date they were going on. It wasn't as though she was about to marry the guy. Not that she could do that anyway seeing she was already married.

"I can't believe you said those things about Joe," Mom continued, sitting back down on the couch and still glaring at me. "Do you really think I would allow you to go on those outings with Joe if I thought he was a criminal or a pedophile? For heaven sake, what kind of a mother do you think I am?"

"You're the greatest mom ever," I said, wanting her to stop glaring at me like that. "I'm sorry if I upset you. Maybe Joe isn't really that bad. Maybe I was mistaken."

Mom kept shaking her head as though she couldn't quite believe we were having this conversation. She must think I've lost my marbles, which is the last thing I wanted her to think. All I wanted to do was get her to think twice about going out with a murderer, or at least a person I was almost sure was a murderer. How had I ever found myself in this pickle? Why hadn't I just told her straight out what I had seen Joe doing that day? She wouldn't have gotten any madder than she already was.

"I fully intend to keep my date with Joe," Mom continued. "If he's any of those things you mentioned, I guess I will be quite safe in a coffee house. The question now is, how am I going to send you out with him again with you thinking he's a criminal of some kind? I was so sure you two had bonded a little bit and that you liked him. Now I'm going to have to request a different person if we're to continue on this program."

"No, that won't be necessary," I insisted. "I can handle it. I really can. I was just concerned about you being alone with him without knowing who he really is."

"He's just a person," Mom said. "A nice person, but nobody you should see as a threat. I want you to like him just like I do. Do you think you can?"

I shrugged and looked away. I didn't want to answer that question. In fact, I didn't want to talk about Joe at all. What I wanted was to have him out of my life and out of my mom's life and the sooner the better.

How I was going to accomplish that, I had no idea.

CHAPTER FIVE

The night Mom went out for coffee with Joe, I was wishing I could be a fly on the wall and listen to what they had to say to each other. I kept looking out my bedroom window waiting for her to return. She seemed to be taking what I considered an awful long time. I mean, how long does it take to have a cup of coffee and a short conversation. Joe didn't have that much to tell Mom because we had only met a couple of times and I hadn't told him a lot. In fact, I had told him practically nothing.

After an hour and she still hadn't come home, I was beginning to panic. What in the world was going on? They sure must be talking about something other than me —that was pretty obvious. What I had feared was happening was what I had tried to warn my mom about. Joe was obviously a smooth operator and no doubt had my mom eating out of his hand. She had assured me that it wasn't really a date at all, just a little get-together to talk about me. How naïve did she think I was anyway?

When she finally did come waltzing in with this little smile on her face, I was pretty put out.

"How come you were gone so long?" I asked her as soon as she got in the door. "I thought you were never coming home."

Mom laughed as she hung up her jacket and then came over and gave me a big hug. "Was my little man worried?" she asked.

"Not really, but it seemed a long time to be having a little chat."

"Well, we got talking," she said leading me over to the couch where we sat beside each other, "and time just seemed to fly. He's such an interesting person and we have so many things in common. He really is a nice guy and you don't need to worry about him being a criminal or a sociopath. I found him really easy to talk to and he said some nice things about you too.

"Like what?"

"Well, he said you were polite and enjoyable to be with. He also thinks you're very smart."

"What gave him that idea? I'm not smart at all. He was probably just trying to butter you up saying stuff like that."

"Ryan, you are very smart. Don't you know that? And I'm quite sure Joe wasn't trying to butter me up. He isn't that kind of person. He's very sincere." She took a deep breath and put her arm around me looking suddenly very serious. "You know what? I think you're being a little possessive of your mom. You don't have to feel as though I'm abandoning you just because I went out for a coffee with somebody. I still love you just as I always have. Nothing will change that."

I was beginning to hate myself, dancing around the subject I wanted most to discuss and not having the courage to do it. I felt so helpless. How could I convince my mom not to go out with Joe any more? It was obvious she wasn't open to any criticism of the guy. She thought he was the greatest and nothing was going to change that.

"Ryan, do you even know what a sociopath is?" my mom asked. "I'm a little amazed that a fifteen-year-old would be talking about a sociopath, let alone my own son. It's not a word I expected to come out of your mouth."

"I found a book in the library on the subject and started reading it. It was really interesting. I didn't know such people existed. I found it a little scary to tell the truth."

My mom shook her head. "What will you be worrying about next?"

I went to camp a few weeks later. I go every year for about three weeks. It's held on Lake Elliot about fifteen miles out of town and it's called Camp Soloman. I like it well enough except this year I had to leave my mom to the mercy of Joe Swenson, the murderer. I didn't like that one bit. Anyway, we do all kinds of things at camp like sailing, swimming, scuba diving and they have a really neat baseball park right beside it where we pick teams and play ball almost every day. Also, the counsellors are good guys to talk to when you've got a problem or something. They're really good listeners.

Before I went to camp, Joe and I went on another bike tour around town and ended up at the zoo. We had quite a laugh at some of the animals that looked like people we knew. There were a couple of monkeys that looked just like my sisters. We both had a big laugh about that. Actually, I was beginning to feel a little guilty mainly because here I was enjoying Joe's company when I should have been giving him the cold shoulder seeing that he was a killer. I felt like I was communing with the enemy.

I didn't want to like Joe, but the more I saw of him, the better I liked him despite what he had done. I honestly tried my best not to like him, but that was hard to do considering that he always took me to the Diary Queen for a malt or a banana split and he made me laugh a lot when he told me jokes. How do you not laugh when a joke is so funny you can't help laughing yourself silly?

Anyway, I phoned my mom every day from camp just to make sure she's doing okay and whether she has gone out with Joe again. I don't actually ask her if she'd seen Joe, I just kind of wait for her to tell me, but she hasn't said anything yet and it's been almost a week.

I had a long talk with Mr. Donaldson, the counsellor, about what I had seen at the beach. He's a great guy and a good listener. After I had had my say, he regarded me with a look that immediately told me that he took what I had said seriously. "This is really bothering you, isn't it?" When I nodded, he leaned forward.

"I haven't heard anything about a murder or a body discovered at the beach, but that doesn't mean much. I don't read the paper very often to be honest so if there was a story about somebody being missing or a possible murder, I might not have been aware of it." He looked at me as though trying to make up his mind whether what I was saying had any merit and if so what he should do. I hadn't told him that I thought the man who carried the woman into the trees was my Big Brother and that we had spent time together.

"So, you didn't go to the police about this and tell them what you saw?"

I shook my head. "I was only twelve at the time. It wasn't until later that I began to realize that what I had seen was maybe a man about to bury somebody he had killed. The more I thought about it, the more I was convinced that that was the case."

"What caused you to start thinking that? Was there something that happened that made you think that perhaps you had witnessed a murder?"

I nodded. "If I tell you what that is, you'll have to promise me that you won't say anything to my mom or anybody about what I tell you. It's pretty shocking."

Mr. Donaldson smiled. "This whole thing is pretty shocking, Ryan. The police should know what you saw though. It might help them to solve a case that by now might be what they call a cold case. But of course, if you don't want me to tell your mom, I certainly will respect your right to privacy. Anything we talk about is strictly between you and me. I would never betray that trust."

"The man I saw carrying the woman into the trees was Joe Swenson, my Big Brother." There, I had said it. I looked at Mr. Donaldson certain that he would be shocked, but his expression didn't change a bit. He just looked at me as though I had told him I hadn't slept very well that night.

"Well, I can see why all this has affected you like it has," he finally said. "And you're certain that the man you saw was your Big Brother?"

I nodded my head. "I'm almost certain. They look the same. I'm pretty good at identifying people."

"Three years is a long time," Mr. Donaldson said. "Our memories aren't always perfect. And you were only twelve years old, a very impressionable age."

"I know, and that's what really bothers me. What if I'm wrong and all this stuff is just a fantasy? I could be worrying for nothing. Maybe that man was taking her into the trees to help her. Maybe she was only sick and had passed out and he was trying to revive her."

"I can see you've been thinking about this a lot. And you've done the right thing to come to me and talk about it. It always helps to talk things through that are bothering us. I'm not sure what to advise you, Ryan. You have certainly been caught up in a dilemma."

"The worse thing is, I think my mom really likes Joe. They even went out together. Mom said it was only for a coffee and to talk about me, but I can tell you I wasn't exactly convinced on that score. I'm afraid she is kind of falling for him and that could be a disaster."

Mr. Donaldson shook his head. "My goodness, this just keeps getting more and more complicated by the minute. What do you think of Joe yourself? Do you like him? Does he strike you as being somebody who is capable of murder?"

"That's what bothers me. He seems like a really nice guy, a regular guy. He's fun to be with and he makes me laugh and then I feel guilty because I know what kind of a person he really is and should I be laughing and having fun with somebody like that? It just doesn't seem right."

"Hmm. I'd say you've got a lot to think about young man. Let's talk about this again and in the meanwhile, I don't think you've got that much to worry about concerning your mom. I know a little about the Big Brothers organization, and they're pretty good at screening the people that represent them."

I went away feeling a little better after finally telling some-body about Joe Swenson. I wondered whether Mr. Donaldson would phone the police and tell them what I had said, but he had promised me that our conversation was strictly confidential.

I phoned Mom that night and she told me that she missed me a lot and that she was going to a movie with Joe Swenson. I almost fell off the chair I was sitting on. What was she thinking?

"Now I know you worry about me, dear, but I want you to know that your old mom can look after herself. I've been around the block a few times and I think I'm a pretty good judge of char-acter. Joe is obviously a nice person who likes me and he likes you and the girls, so why shouldn't I trust him?"

"But Mom, he—"

"He could be a psychopath? Well, I guess he could be, but don't you think it's a lot more likely that he's just a nice man. I've already talked to a couple of the girls who knew him in high school and they say he's a great guy. So, relax and enjoy camp and have fun."

How was I supposed to have fun when my own mother was going to the movies with a…a suspected psychopath? And who was looking after my sisters while mom was gadding about with Joe, going to the movies and who knows what else.? Well, I guess Angela was old enough to baby sit. She was almost thirteen, going on ten. It seemed like asking for trouble having Angela look after her sister when all they did was argue.

I tried to enjoy the rest of my time at camp, but I kept think-ing about Mom going out with Joe. Surely, she couldn't be serious about him. She had never seemed interested in anybody except my dad and now that he was gone forever, I would have thought she would forget about relationships. Not that she was too old, but she didn't seem as though a relationship with another man was something she was interested in. Not until now, that is.

When I finally arrived home (one of the counsellors dropped me off) I could see Joe's truck parked out in front, his bike sticking out the back.

Holy Hanna, had the guy moved in or what? Was I destined to have Joe Swenson around my neck forever? What would I have to do in order to discourage him from coming around?

Mom was at the door almost as soon as I dropped my bag and hung up my jacket. "Well, look who's here," she said, beaming, as though everything was right with the world now that I had come home safe and sound. She put her arms around me and gave me the biggest hug ever. "I've missed you so much, Ryan. It's wonderful to have you home again. I hope you really enjoyed camp." She gave me this mysterious look. "You'll never guess who's here."

Oh yes, I would. Before I could open my mouth, my two sisters made an appearance and stood staring at me as though I was a stranger. When I rolled my eyes, they both giggled and ran back into the front room where no doubt Joe was holding court and amusing my mom and my sisters like he was one of the family.

"I have no idea," I told my mom. I was sure that was the answer she wanted. My mom always liked to surprise me, but this time there was no surprise at all.

"Mr. Swenson, your Big Brother, is here. You must have seen his truck outside."

My Big Brother! As if I had forgotten that for heaven sake. I had only been gone three weeks. You would think I had lost my memory or something.

"Nice to see you again, Ryan," Joe said as I entered the front room. He came up to me and held out his hand. "Welcome back. It seems like you've been gone forever. I think those sisters of yours missed you almost as much as your mom."

I shook his hand, wanting to disappear through the floorboards. And that crack about my sisters missing me. What a joke. If they never saw me again, ever, they would probably be practically hysterical with glee.

"Now you sit right down," Mom said. "We're having some lemonade. Would you like some?"

I shook my head. "I'm pretty full. They feed you really good at camp." All I wanted to do was head for my room and get away from the goofy stares of my sisters and Joe and enjoy a little solitude. I had a lot to think about and the sooner I got onto to it, the better.

"Well, you can tell us all about camp. I'm sure Joe will be interested." She smiled over at him and I wanted nothing more than to throw up. If that look didn't have a whole lot of meaning, then my name isn't Ryan Sinclair. She came over and sat down beside me, put her arm around me, all the time smiling like a Cheshire Cat. "Oh, I could squeeze you to death. And you've got such a nice tan. Don't you think so, girls?"

My sisters didn't say anything. They just sat there looking at me, probably wondering why Mom was making such a fuss over me instead of them.

But I was glad to see my mom again and it was good to see her looking so happy. I couldn't help wondering though, if that happiness was because of my coming home or because Joe was sitting there like he belonged here.

"So, what did you like the best about being at camp?" Joe suddenly asked.

I wanted to tell him my talk with Mr. Donaldson headed the list, but I'm quite sure that wasn't what he wanted to hear. It was true, though, I really enjoyed talking to Mr. Donaldson. He was such a good listener and seemed really interested in what I had to say. And even though he wasn't able to solve my little dilemma, at least his advice gave me something to think about.

"Sitting around the campfire at night with my friends, roasting wieners and marshmallows. Some of the counsellors were pretty good at telling ghost stories that scared the dickens out of us. I didn't like having to get up so early in the morning, though. I guess I'm going to have to catch up on my sleep now that I'm home." I managed a big fake yawn hoping that Mom might take the hint and send me off to my room to catch up on my sleep. She was always worried about me not getting enough rest. I looked over at her with the most mournful look I could muster, but she just smiled back at me as though she knew what I was up to.

"You've got all week to catch up on your sleep, dear," she said.

So much for that idea. I spent the next half-hour listening to my sister moan about not being able to go to camp and how much work they had to do around the house much to the amusement of Joe. He kept shaking his head as though he couldn't quite believe that two little girls who had the most privileged lifestyle imaginable could come up with so many complaints.

After what I considered a decent amount of time, I yawned again and looked at my mom. "I think I'll just retire to my room," I told her. "I'm really bushed. I need to lay down for a bit, catch my breath."

My mom laughed. "Boy, they must be really putting you through your paces at camp these days," she said. "It's a good thing it was only for three weeks, otherwise I might have to admit you to the medical centre and have them check you over. I think Joe was hoping to have a little talk with you since you haven't seen each other for over three weeks."

"Hey, that's quite all right. We can talk some other time when you're feeling a little more chipper." Joe glanced at his watch. "Besides, I've got an appointment in about half-an-hour."

He waved goodbye and mom saw him off at the door. It seemed to me it was taking them an awful long time to separate from each other. I wondered what they were doing. My sisters were giggling like a couple of gaggling geese as though they knew something I didn't know.

I escaped to my room where I was finally able to relax without having to listen to my sisters and explain to everybody how wonderful camp was when I really could have done without it. I enjoyed being home more than anywhere else, but Mom always thought I would benefit from mixing with other boys my age. She was really into the socializing thing. I guess she was concerned that I was going to turn into a hermit since I didn't have many friends and spent a lot of time by myself.

I didn't see Joe for another week during which I had done a lot of thinking. Mom was her usual self and didn't say a lot, but I knew things had changed in her life and not for the good as far as I was concerned.

Joe took me to the museum. It was amazing that I had lived in our town all my life and I had never visited our museum. I was quite impressed with how much Joe knew about the things we looked at. No matter what else he might be, a murderer for instance, he was no dummy. He had a lot of information stored in his head and wasn't shy about sharing it with me. I was quite sure even my teachers didn't know as much as Joe did.

It wasn't until we went to the Dairy Queen for our usual treat, the Joe told me he wanted to talk to me about something quite serious. I was totally convinced he was going to confess about killing that girl down at the beach, but that wasn't it. What he wanted to talk about was his relationship with my mom. Horror of horrors. Did I really want to hear this?

"The fact is," he began, "that your mom and I...well, we've started dating and I wanted to feel you out and find out what you think of that. After all, you kids will be affected by our relationship and I just want to be certain that you have no objections. Your mom and I have a lot in common. We even went to the same school. Imagine that. And she's a wonderful person, but you already know that. Right?"

As horrified as I was, I hadn't expected this. What did he expect me to say for heaven sakes? Oh yes, I'm delighted that you, a suspected killer, are going to be dating my mom. What a wonderful surprise. Do you plan to take her down to the beach and carry her unconscious into the trees just like you had that other woman? I wanted to scream bloody murder right there in the Dairy Queen, but I didn't. I held my tongue and tried my best not to look as horrified as I felt. I mean, what in the world was going on? And what could I possibly do to prevent this?

"I know this must come as a bit of a shock to you," Joe continued. "Actually, it's quite a shock to me. I hadn't expected this to happen. But your mom is such an exceptional person that I... well, I just kind of fell in love with her. It's not every day I meet somebody like your mom."

When I didn't say anything since I was totally speechless, I guess he felt compelled to fill in the silence. "If you want, I can arrange to have somebody else be your Big Brother since this could be seen as a conflict of interests if you know what I mean."

He smiled across at me. "It would sure mean a lot to me if you kind of gave me a hint that you approve of what your mom and I are doing." When I still hadn't said anything. I was literally bowled over. I couldn't ever remember being in a more awkward position. Finally, he reached across the table and patted me on the arm. "So, what do you say? Have we got your blessing? We already talked to your sisters and they seemed quite accepting."

"My dad might come home some day," I told him. I didn't know what else to say. If the truth were known, I wanted to discourage him. It didn't want my mom associated with a possible murderer. What if they decided to get married or if Mom asked him to move in with us. What a calamity that would be.

"Your mom and I talked about that. Your dad has been gone a long time. I think the chances of him returning are pretty remote. Your mom wants to get on with her life and I think she deserves that. After all, she isn't that old and I really believe we're a great match."

"What would you do if my dad did come home?" I suddenly asked him.

He laughed. "I guess that would be a little awkward, wouldn't it? But your mom has already assured me that should he return, it's extremely unlikely that they could ever live as man and wife again.

It just isn't in the cards." He paused, waiting for a response. When I didn't say anything, he continued. "How do you feel about your dad returning?"

I shrugged. "I don't know. It would be kind of weird I guess. After four years I might not even recognize him. But he is my dad. I guess I should be glad if he returned but I'm not sure about that."

"I can understand how you must feel."

"You and Mom can't get married since she's already married to my dad. Right?"

"Right. But you don't have to worry about that. We're just dating, Ryan. We aren't to the point of making any kind of commitment to each other. That might come later after we know each other better and you and your sisters feel comfortable having me around."

I never did give Joe my okay concerning him dating my mom. I'm not sure whether he was disappointed or what, because he didn't say anything about it and he didn't look all that upset. Maybe he thought he could work on me in the coming days and that I would eventually weaken and give in and tell him how happy I was that he and mom were now an item. Since he had recruited my two simple little sisters, who were too starry-eyed about him to object to anything he said, he probably thought I would eventually come around. I had news for him. Considering what I knew about him, it's a wonder I even entertained the idea of going anywhere with him let alone giving him the idea that he could maybe be my substitute father.

Later, in my room, I thought about my conversation with Joe at the Dairy Queen. If only I hadn't seen what I had seen at the beach. My opinion of Joe would be so much different. I mean, he seemed to be such a nice guy, but knowing what I knew about him made it really hard to like him and especially hard accepting him as my mom's boyfriend. Mom should know what she was getting into, but I just wasn't prepared to tell her. It seemed like an impossible task to me. She had already been hurt when my dad left and now I had to tell her that her new boyfriend was a possible murderer? How could I do that? If I only knew for certain that I was right, that the man I had seen at the beach was really Joe. It would make my little task a whole lot easier that's for sure.

How in the world would I ever find out for certain whether Joe was that man? There were a number of options open to me. I could ask him, but that was completely out of the question. Of course, he would deny it. What killer ever confessed to their crime? I could go to the police, but they would just laugh at me. I could go back to where he might have buried that lady and look some more, but I had pretty well exhausted that option.

And then an idea occurred to me that I thought just might work. It was a little bit sneaky and maybe a long shot, but who knew? I was desperate and I needed to know.

CHAPTER SIX

It wasn't until almost a week later that Joe showed up to take me on another outing. Before he had a chance to suggest anything, I told him I wanted to go back to the beach, near where my fort had been.

"Oh? Okay." He looked as though wondering why I would want to do that since we had already been there, but I just gave him a smile and headed for the door before he could suggest something different.

We hopped on our bikes and off we went. It was about a half-hour trip on our bikes. It was a perfect day, not too hot and with a nice gentle breeze. I felt totally in control and was looking forward to being in a place that had once been my favorite spot in the world. I was also looking forward to how Joe would react. If we were returning to the scene of his crime, he might give himself away in some manner and I would feel more confident that he was the killer.

When we got there, I stopped right in front of where my fort had been at one time and got off my bike. I stood looking into the trees trying to see whether there was anything left of my little fort. After over three years, it didn't seem likely.

"Is this where your little hideout used to be?" he asked, looking into the trees and then back at me. He didn't look in any way, guilty or upset. If this was where he had committed his crime, he was certainly a good actor, because he just grinned over at me, got off his bike and approached the trees where I was standing.

"Where was your hideout exactly?" he asked.

I pointed it out, but there wasn't much to see. I watched him closely, but if he was guilty of anything, he wasn't giving it away. What a disappointment. But I wasn't ready to give up yet. Where he had carried the woman into the trees was maybe twenty or thirty yards up from where my fort used to be. Maybe I could make Joe a little more nervous as I began walking closer to where I remembered he had carried the woman.

Joe followed me, looking a little confused. "Did you have another fort up here?" he asked, looking around.

I shook my head. "No, it's just a spot I was originally thinking about having my fort, but I finally decided that it was a little too open. I wanted a place where nobody could see me."

"Oh. Well, that makes sense…I guess."

I walked into the trees as though looking for something. Joe didn't follow me in, just stood watching me as though wondering what I was up to. I made a big show of looking around in there, and when I came out, Joe was sitting on the sand looking out over the lake.

"This is really a nice spot," he said. "I can see why you wanted a fort and liked to spend time here. This area used to be a kind of lover's lane a long time ago when I was a kid. But I guess the kids have found another place because hardly anybody ever comes here any more."

If I thought my little ruse was going to convince me of Joe's guilt, it was a total bust as far as I was concerned. Joe hadn't shown any sign that he was the one who had murdered that girl. He didn't seem nervous at all. I just had to assume that he had nerves of steel or was a good actor.

Back at the Dairy Queen an hour later, Joe scratched his head and looked at me a little puzzled. "You like going back to your old hide-out, don't you? It must have been a happy time for you. Right?"

I shrugged. "I guess."

"I had a tree house once that I liked hiding in when I wanted to get away from everything. It gave me a real feeling of comfort and a chance to relax and not have to think about all the things that were bothering me. So, I know how you must feel about your fort."

Boy, I thought, this guy must be really good at self-denial. I was having a hard time believing anything he said, but he sure sounded logical and if he was a murderer, it didn't seem to be bothering him very much. Of course, from what I had read about sociopaths, their crimes were just like water off a duck's back. They didn't have a conscience at all and were very good at convincing people how wonderful they were.

'You've had a little time to think about your mom and I getting together. I sure was hoping you might give me your blessing. I would hate to think that you were hoping that I might suddenly disappear from the scene or anything like that. The more I see of your mom, the better I like her. She's a great lady." He leaned toward me and gave me a big phoney smile. "Have you had any thoughts about me seeing your mom?"

I didn't want to tell him anything. Well, that wasn't quite true. I would like to have told him to make himself scarce or better still, admit what he had done, tell my mother so she could see what a horrible person he was. But that obviously wasn't going to happen.

"I guess it's okay," I finally said, hating myself for not being able to say what I really felt. But there didn't seem to be any point in making things difficult. For one thing, Joe would probably want to know why I didn't like him when we had spent so much time together and I seemed to be enjoying myself.

"I think your mom likes me as well," Joe continued. He grinned across at me. "I guess you're too young to have a girlfriend, but one day you'll know what I mean when I say how smitten I am with your mom. It's not very often that I meet somebody I like the way I like her. Can you understand that?"

"I guess so," I said, trying my best to look disinterested.

A few weeks later, I went back to school still worried about my mom and her romance with Joe. It seemed as though Joe was coming over to our house more and more often and not just to see me, but to go on a date with my mom. I tried my best to think of what I could do to break them up, but I couldn't come up with anything. I even talked it over with Arnie, but he didn't have any ideas either.

"You're just going to have to accept the fact that your mom is dating a killer. I guess there's worse things, but I can't think of any."

"Thanks a lot," I told him. "You've just made my day."

"Hey, I'm only trying to help. Besides, he probably isn't a killer anyway. Your best option is to give the guy a break and accept him for what he is: a nice guy who is dating your mom and hoping to become your new dad."

"Sometimes I wonder why I even talk to you, Arnie. You're about as helpful as a blow on the head."

He laughed. "Think of it this way. You are about to have your missing dad replaced by a much nicer guy. Right? You told me your dad ignored you like you had the plague."

"Wrong. Well, maybe right if he turns out not to be a killer I guess. But that seems like a long shot. I saw him, remember. He wasn't more than a stone's throw away from me. I got a good look at him. It's the same guy. I've got a really good memory for faces."

Arnie shook his head. "That's what they all say. I'll bet before you met poor old Joe that you couldn't pick him out of a lineup if your life depended on it. Oh, and by the way, how is the Big Brother thing going? Are you two still an item or have they replaced Joe with somebody else considering he's hot on the trail of your mom?"

"He's still my Big Brother—unfortunately. But I guess I can't really complain. He's been a good friend and we've been all over the place together and he's easy to talk to." I sighed. "What do you think of that? Here I am a good friend to a killer who is courting my mom and spending time with me, acting as though he's my dad. What kind of a dilemma is that?"

"It's one I don't want," Arnie said.

CHAPTER SEVEN

Over the next few months I tried my best to just not think of what was going on in my life, but I wasn't very successful. Every time I turned around, it seemed Joe was in my face, smiling as though everything was right with the world. I guess he was happy. He had a girlfriend and they seemed to be hitting it off really well. And I seemed to be doing more baby-sitting by the day. The only good thing about the baby-sitting was that Mom would slip me the odd ten- dollar bill. It was nice to have the extra money but having to put up with my two sisters barely made up for it.

It wasn't until November that my dad returned. It was a cold day with a brisk wind, the kind of day you just want to hunker down somewhere, preferably in front of the fireplace, when there he was. As big as life. And he hadn't changed much which is surprising considering I hadn't seen him for over four years. He was standing beside his car, the same one he had left in, in front of the school, when I came out with Arnie.

"Hey, isn't that your old man?" Arnie said. I was surprised that Arnie recognized him because he hadn't seen him for a long time.

My dad waved me over to his car. I looked at Arnie and rolled my eyes. "Can you believe this?"

"Let's go over and hear what he has to say. This should be interesting."

Dad was smoking a cigarette as we approached but flicked it away and grinned at me. "Hey, kid, how are you doing? Are you glad to see your old dad?"

I was speechless, but Arnie wasn't. "Hey Mr. Sinclair, how are you? Long time no see."

My dad glanced at Arnie and made a face. I got the distinct impression that he would have preferred that I was alone. I was glad that Arnie was with me.

"How come you came back?" I couldn't think of anything else to say.

"You've really grown, kid. I hardly recognized you." It was obvious he wasn't going to answer my question. "How's your mom?"

"She's okay. She's got a boyfriend now. He's my Big Brother."

"Oh." Dad looked deflated as though my statement had let out all the air in his body. "I guess it isn't anything serious though."

"I wouldn't say that. They seem pretty serious to me. He spends more time at our house than I do."

My dad didn't seem too pleased about that. "I thought I would come and pick you up at school so we could talk before going home to your mom."

"She's not going to be too happy to see you," I said. I looked over at Arnie. He was grinning from ear to ear, fully enjoying our conversation.

"Why do you say that?" My dad asked.

I could hardly believe what he had said. I mean, here my dad had left town without a word, stayed away for four years and now couldn't understand why my mom wouldn't be happy to see him.

"Well, for one thing, she's got a new boyfriend and for another, you've been gone for a long time. She didn't think you were ever coming back."

Dad looked at Arnie and scowled. "Why don't you get lost, Arnie. Ryan and I have to have a little talk—strictly private if you know what I mean."

"I was hoping for a ride home," Arnie said, giving me a forlorn look that I knew was about as real as a three-legged cat. I also knew that Arnie was dying to hear what my dad was going to say.

"Can't we give Arnie a ride?" I appealed to my dad. "He's my friend, my best friend."

"What? Is he lame or something. It's only six blocks to his house."

"It's quite a bit further than that."

Dad looked exasperated. "Oh, all right, hop in."

We both went around to the other side of the car and I got in the front seat beside my dad while Arnie got in the back seat.

"How is your mom, anyway?" Dad asked as we pulled away from the curb.

"She seems pretty happy these days what with a new boy-friend and all. She was really depressed for a long time after you left."

"Yeah, I meant to write and tell her what happened, but I never seemed to be able to get around to it. I'm not much of a letter writer."

"You could have phoned," I countered.

"Yeah, I guess I could have. I'm really sorry about that. I hope your mom will forgive me."

"She's going to be really shocked when you show up," I said. "I mean, really shocked."

"You've been gone a long time, Mr. Sinclair. Things change, people change." Arnie grinned at me. If there was one thing Arnie enjoyed, it was a little controversy. I had learned that after paling around with him all these years.

Dad was quiet for several minutes as we drove along. When we got close to Arnie's place, he pulled over. "Here you are, kid. See you later."

"I'm impressed," Arnie said, "that you remember where I live. Good memory. See you tomorrow, Ryan. Don't take any wooden nickels."

As we pulled away, Dad turned to me. "I'm surprised you still hang around with that guy. A real loser."

"Who, Arnie?" I asked, feigning surprise. "He's a real nice guy. He's got a great sense of humor and he's really smart."

"I'll bet," Dad said. "Anyway, I sure hope your mom is okay with me coming back. What do you think, Ryan?"

"She might not let you in the house," I said. "She's pretty mad."

Dad laughed nervously. "Well, I've got news for her. It's my house too. Just because I left for awhile, doesn't mean I gave up owning the house."

As we got close to home, I could see Joe's truck parked in our driveway. This was definitely an unfortunate development—at least for my dad.

"Joe's here," I said.

"Who's Joe?" Dad asked.

"Mom's boyfriend. He's a real nice guy. He's my Big Brother."

Dad pulled over to the curb and stopped. "Your big brother? What in the hell is that?"

"It's an association. You know, guys who volunteer to be mentors for kids like me who don't have a father."

"Great. This is all I need. Some do-gooder trying to take my place. Probably thinks he owns the place since I haven't been around."

"He's not like that," I explained, suddenly wondering why I was defending a murderer. Or at least somebody I thought was a murderer.

"Don't tell me he's got you fooled too." Dad threw up his arms. "Any other surprises I should be aware of." He looked at me with the most disgusting look on his face. Suddenly, I wasn't sure I wanted to be in the middle of this whole thing. Why couldn't he have stayed away instead of coming back and making our lives even more complicated than they already were?

"What do you want me to do? Mom isn't going to be happy seeing you when her boyfriend is over visiting."

"Go in and tell him to get lost. Once he's gone, I'll come in and talk some sense to your mom. Okay?"

I shrugged. "O.K."

I got out of his car and walked up the driveway to our house. By the time I got to the door, I could see mom looking out.

"Who is that?" she wanted to know as soon as I had opened the front door. I could see Joe sitting in the living room with my two sisters.

"It's Dad. He's back. He picked me up at school and drove me home. I think he wants to come in and talk to you."

Mom suddenly looked very pale, as though someone had delivered the worst possible news imaginable. "Oh my god," she said. "What is he doing here? I can't believe this." She looked at me and then back at Joe sitting in the living room. "You've got to tell him I don't want to see him. He can't come in right now. Can you do that, Ryan?"

"I told him about Joe," I said. "He wants you to get rid of him and then he'll come in and talk to you."

"No, I don't want that. I don't want to talk to him at all. Oh my god, what am I supposed to do? I don't want to talk to him."

"Is everything all right, Marjorie?" Joe said from the living room.

"Honey, you go right out there and tell your dad I don't want to see him." She gave me a hug. "I'm sorry to put you in the middle of this, but I can't have him coming in here right now."

The last thing I wanted to do was tell my dad he couldn't come into his own house, but what else could I do? I felt like I was trapped somehow. How come all this was coming down on me?

I looked at my mom and shrugged. "Okay, but he's not going to like it."

I walked back out to dad's car. He was sitting there smoking a cigarette with a distinctive scowl on his face. I got in and sat down and rolled down the window. I didn't like the smell of cigarette smoke.

"She doesn't want to see you," I told him.

"Oh really." My dad stared at me as though I was the one who was preventing him from coming into his own house. I wanted to tell him that I was only the messenger, but I don't think he was prepared to hear that. "Well, you go back in there and tell her I'm coming in whether she wants me to or not. I don't care whether her boyfriend is there. That's just too bad. I want to see the girls for starters and that's still my house. Just because I left for awhile doesn't give her the right to refuse to let me come in."

"I can't do that," I said, beginning to feel sick to my stomach. I'm not sure whether it was from the smoke in the car or the tense situation. All I wanted to do was get as far away from this whole thing as I could and not have to think about it any more. But I knew that wasn't going to happen.

Dad just glared at me. "What's wrong with you? Can't you go and deliver a simple message? I'm your dad, remember."

I got out of the car and ran up the stairs to the front door. When I opened it, Mom and Joe were standing there.

"What did he say?" Mom asked me.

"He said he's coming in whether you like it or not." I headed for my room. I was finished being the messenger. I just wanted to be alone in my room and not have to think about anything. As far as I was concerned, it wasn't my problem. So why was I the one who was caught in the middle, the one who had to deliver all the messages that nobody wanted to hear?

Once in my room, I put my earphones on and lay on my bed listening to Bon Jovi but not really hearing him. I was visualizing myself on a quiet beach somewhere enjoying the sound of the surf and the swaying of palm trees and the gentle breeze coming off the ocean. I was miles away and I didn't have to even think about what was going on in my life.

I don't know how much later, my mom knocked on my door and came into my room. She sat down on my bed beside me. I felt badly that I had coped out, but I didn't know what else to do. I took off my earphones and looked over at her. She smiled down at me and then leaned over and kissed me on the top of my head.

"I'm sorry you got caught up in the middle of all this, Ryan." She sighed heavily, looking more upset than I had ever seen her. "Everybody's gone. Joe went home and your dad drove away, thank heavens. I just wasn't up to talking to him."

"What are you going to do?" I asked her.

She sighed again. "I don't know. I can scarcely believe your dad has come back. Why now all of a sudden after being away all these years? It doesn't make any sense to me."

"Does he still own our house? Can he just come in if we don't want him to?"

"I guess he can. I don't know. I might have to contact a lawyer. Surely deserting us for over three years means something."

When we left my room and went out to the living room where my sisters were watching TV, they both turned to us looking confused.

"Was that our dad," Angela wanted to know, "sitting out in that car?"

"I'm afraid it was," Mom said.

"Why didn't he come in?"

Mom looked over at me and then back to Angela. "Because I didn't want him to. Maybe you'll be able to see him later. Would you like that?"

The girls looked at one another and then nodded their heads.

Dad didn't return the next day nor the day after that. I think both Mom and I were relieved there wasn't going to be a confrontation. Joe and Mom talked a lot about what was going on. I could hear them from my room. Of course, I couldn't hear what they were actually saying, but I could well imagine that it had a lot to do with my dad returning.

The next day when I came out of the school with Arnie, I was on the lookout for Dad's car, but I didn't see it, much to my relief. I'm not sure Arnie was so disappointed though. He was very curious about what was going to happen. Nothing this dramatic ever happened at his house.

"So, what do you think is going to happen?" he asked me. "Do you think your dad has done the old disappearing act again?"

I shrugged. "Who knows. He seemed like he was determined to come into our house just as though he had never left. I'm kind of surprised he hasn't shown up."

"Oh, he'll show up all right. Just like a bad penny."

I was constantly amused by Arnie. Actually, I was kind of glad to have him as a constant companion these days. It made the possibility of running into my dad a little less stressful. He presented a whole different aspect to my dad. He almost welcomed the thought of running into him while I dreaded it. Also, Arnie had a way with words that I definitely did not. I was somewhat speechless when it came to trying to talk to my dad whereas Arnie just dove right in where angels feared to tread.

After about a week and my dad hadn't shown up again, I began to hope that maybe he had gone back to wherever he had been for the last three years. I was so caught up in the dramatic appearance of my dad, that I hadn't thought very much about Joe and his part in a murder. How had my life become so complicated so suddenly? And what was I to do now? Just accept Joe knowing what I knew? If I had been on good terms with my dad, I could have explained everything to him, but there was no way I was going to confide in him considering how Mom felt. It was quite obvious she felt threatened and caught up in a situation that could quite easily turn nasty.

CHAPTER EIGHT

One Saturday about two weeks after my incident with my dad, I biked over to the local mall. Mom wanted me to pick up some groceries for her. I had a basket that fitted on the front of my bike so that whenever I needed to carry anything, I just had to attach it to the handlebars. The mall was only about a half-mile from our house and since Arnie's house was on my way, I stopped and asked him if he wanted to come with me. He eagerly agreed. There was an arcade in the mall that Arnie particularly liked where we sometimes idled away a few hours when we didn't have anything better to do.

Unfortunately, on this day, as we walked along looking into the stores and enjoying the aroma of the cinnamon shop, I spied my dad sitting by himself on a bench. Before I had a chance to turn around and go the other way, he saw me and waved us over.

This was all I needed to spoil my Saturday, but I could hardly ignore him even though that was precisely what I wanted to do.

"Hey, kid, what are you up to?" he asked, as we approached him. To me he looked quite pathetic to be honest. I almost felt sorry for him.

"Hi Mr. Sinclair," Arnie said, sitting down beside him. "How're things going?"

Dad just looked at him and didn't say anything. "What are you doing here?" he asked again, looking up at me.

"Mom wanted a few things," I told him, holding up my little shopping list.

"Well, how about sitting down and talking to your old man," he said, moving over so that there was room for me to sit between Arnie and him. "I've been meaning to get over and see the girls and talk to your mom, but I've been busy."

I wondered what he had been busy about. He had probably been spending time at his favorite pub and seeing some of his old drinking buddies. Sometimes I had to wonder at his priorities. He had come back home after being absent for over three years and hadn't even seen his two little girls yet. Hmm? What was one supposed to think about that?

"I've been wanting to ask you about this guy your mom's been going out with. What's his name? Joe something?"

"Swenson," Arnie said. "From what I hear, he's a real nice guy."

"Is that right?" Dad looked over at me. "So, what do you know about him? Hell, he could be some kind of con man. Knowing your mom and how naïve she is, any guy could show up on her doorstep and have her eating out of his hand. I don't like it at all and I especially don't like him spending a whole lot of time in my house with my wife. Know what I mean, Ryan?"

I nodded. "Arnie's right. He seems like a nice guy. I don't think Mom would go out with a con man. She's a pretty good judge of character."

My dad laughed. "Are you kidding? Your mom...well, maybe I shouldn't say too much. I know how she dotes on you and the girls."

"He's part of the Big Brother's Association too," Arnie put in. "They don't just recruit anybody. You have to be pretty respectable before they sign you up."

"How the hell would you know that?" My dad glared at Arnie. "How would a fifteen-year-old kid know anything about the Big Brothers? They're just like all these other associations. They're hard up for candidates so they just practically pull people

80

off the street. I sure don't want my son and especially my own wife associating with one of them."

"Maybe if you met him, you might change your mind," Arnie said. "From what I could see, he seemed like a really good guy. I don't think you have to worry about your wife. She's in good hands."

I wanted to strangle Arnie. He was pushing the envelope a little bit far. And I knew that considering my dad's temper, he wasn't going to like what Arnie had said.

"Why don't you take a little walk, Arnie," Dad said, glaring at my friend like he would like to stifle him on the spot. "I need to talk to my son without being interrupted every minute."

Arnie grinned. "I'll take a stroll down to the arcade. Real nice seeing you again, Mr. Sinclair. Why don't you join me, Ryan, once you and your dad have had your little talk?"

We both watched as Arnie walked down the mall, looking in the windows of stores and when he turned and saw us looking at him, he held up his thumb in a kind of go get him gesture.

"That kid drives me crazy," my dad said. "He needs to learn some manners. If he was my kid, I'd smarten him up real fast."

"He's okay," I said. "He doesn't really mean to be rude or anything. It's just the way he is."

Dad just shook his head as though he didn't believe a word I said. "Anyway, I'm worried about you and the girls. I don't like the idea of this guy Joe moving in on you guys. Like I said, he could be anything."

"He hasn't moved in," I corrected him. "He just comes over sometimes. He and Mom go out on dates the odd time and I baby-sit. It's no big deal." I could just imagine what my dad would be saying if I told him I thought Joe was a murderer. He definitely would go ballistic.

"He might seem like a wonderful guy to an impressionable fifteen-year-old, but for my money the guy's after something. I know your mom inherited some money from your grandparents.

He probably knows that and sees your mom as a meal ticket. I'm going to have to have a talk to her, talk some sense into that head of hers."

"I don't think he's like that. And he's got a good job. He teaches phys-ed at the senior high school."

"A teacher, huh? That's all she needs. Some of the teachers I know aren't worth the powder to blow them to hell. That's worse than him being one of those scum bag lawyers."

I laughed to myself. Even if I had told my dad that Joe was a Sunday School teacher, he probably would have said something derogatory about them.

"Anyway, you tell your mom that I'll be around to see her pretty soon. We got to get some things straight. You know what I mean?"

"Like what?" I asked.

"Never you mind. I'll talk to your mom and get her straightened around about some things. You needn't bother your head about them."

"I got to go and get some groceries," I told him, standing up. "I think Mom needs them for supper."

"You be sure and give her my message." He glared at me. "And tell your sisters I'll be over to see them too. I've sure missed those little girls."

I'll bet you did, I thought, as I made my way down to join Arnie at the arcade. My dad leaves for four years and then comes home and he still hasn't seen my sisters. What a joke. If he really missed them, he wouldn't have left in the first place, and since he had returned, he hadn't made any real effort to come over and see them. Just what kind of a father was he?

"So, how did it go?" Arnie wanted to know when I joined him at the arcade. He

was playing some crazy war game that required his undivided attention. "I'll bet he

was all over our guy Joe like a wet blanket. Am I right?"

"He thinks Joe is some kind of con man."

"Well, at least he doesn't think he's a murderer which he could well be."

"I didn't dare tell him about Joe carrying that woman into the trees. He probably would have made a bee-line for the cop shop."

After I had gotten the groceries Mom needed, Arnie and I pedalled back to his house. "See you on Monday," Arnie said. "That is if your dad hasn't run Joe off the property or blown up your house."

I laughed. "I don't think that's very likely. But I'm a little scared about him coming over and hassling my mom. I wish he would just make a disappearing act like he did the first time. It would sure make everything a lot simpler."

"That's like wishing the moon was made out of cheese. Good luck with that."

Arnie wasn't exactly the most optimistic person I knew, but he could be pretty realistic at times.

When I got home, I told Mom about seeing Dad in the mall. She looked at me as though seeing him was about the most traumatic thing I could endure.

"What did he say?" she wanted to know.

I told her everything about our little conversation. She wasn't happy about him coming over. "Me and the girls are just going to have to arrange to be out of the house when he comes. Did he say when he's planning his little visit?"

I shook my head. "I got the impression it was going to be soon though."

That night Joe came over. He wanted to know if I could come with him while he bought a boat that he had seen for sale in the paper. "I'm a pretty good bargainer so you might learn something about not offering what the seller is asking. You could save a heck of a lot of money some day. Besides, I want to talk to you about a few things."

I was a little afraid about leaving Mom in case my dad came over while we were away. There was no telling what he would say to her to upset her.

"Don't you worry about me," Mom said, suspecting why I was hesitating. "I'll take the girls out for a little drive. I still need time to think about what I'm going to do about him."

I shrugged. "Okay…I guess." I wasn't sure I wanted to go anywhere with Joe, but the thought of being here if my dad showed up wasn't something I cared to be around for. And I knew Mom liked the idea of Joe and me spending time together.

"Maybe we could stop at the Dairy Queen for a little treat. What do you think, girls? Would you like that?"

The girls squealed their approval in unison.

"I think your mom is really worried about your dad coming over," Joe said as he drove toward the marina where he hoped to buy a boat. "I think she's a little frightened of him. What do you think, Ryan? Do you think she's got anything to worry about?"

I shrugged. "I don't know. I can't remember him hurting her before he left. All I know is that he drank a lot of beer and sometimes would come home late at night after the rest of us had gone to bed, stumbling over furniture and throwing things around. And doing a lot of cursing."

"How do you feel about your dad? Would you like to see him come home and live with you again?"

I wasn't sure what I wanted. And since my dad had been gone so long, the thought of him coming back just as though nothing had happened, didn't make much sense to me. Besides, it was pretty obvious Mom didn't want him back either. I think she had fallen out of love with him after three years and now, with a new boyfriend, things were a lot different in her life. She wanted to move on and I agreed with that idea.

"No," I said. "I guess it would be nice to have a dad again, but he was never much of a dad before he left. And I don't think he's changed much."

"I'm glad your mom is taking the girls out. I don't like the idea of your dad coming over when I'm not there."

I had practically forgotten about Joe being a possible murderer. What was worse? Keeping company with a killer or having to put up with my dad who seemed to be on the warpath and ready for combat. Talk about a choice between two evils. Well, at least Joe was good company and not negative all the time like my dad was, even if he was a murderer. I wondered whether I would ever know the truth about him. The image of him carrying that woman into the trees seemed indelibly stamped into my psyche. I dreamed about it and had it on my mind constantly. It was like a monkey on my back that I longed to be rid of.

CHAPTER NINE

I was impressed with Joe, the way he negotiated with the seller of the sail boat he was interested in. It looked like he had saved himself about ten thousand dollars and it only took him a matter of a few minutes before the two men shook hands and Joe was the new owner of a thirty-eight- foot sail boat.

"So, did you learn anything?" he wanted to know as we drove back to our house.

I rolled my eyes. I hadn't ever tried bargaining for anything in my life, so what Joe had done, was completely new to me. "Very impressive…I guess, since you saved a bunch of money. I don't know whether I could do that or not."

Joe laughed. "It's all a matter of practice. And knowing your prices. I knew right away he was asking too much for the boat. I think he knew that, but in the end, he seemed pretty happy with the price I offered."

When we got back to the house, there was my dad banging on the front door and peering into the front window to see if anybody was home. Thank heavens Mom was still out with my sisters.

"Oh, oh, this is not good," I said.

Joe parked on the street and we both got out of his truck and walked toward the house. Joe grinned over at me as though he was looking forward to confronting my dad. I was a little taken aback by that, I must admit.

"Mister Sinclair," Joe said as we approached him. He held out his hand. "Joe Swenson. How are you doing today?"

My dad didn't look one bit happy, but almost reluctantly, shook Joe's hand. "I'm looking for—" He turned to me, "your mother. I knocked but nobody answered."

"She took my sisters for a drive," I told him. "They might not be back for hours."

"Would you like to come inside and wait?" Joe asked, still grinning and seeming to be enjoying himself. I was almost certain he knew that my dad wasn't about to come in and wait for my mom.

My dad looked around and then back at Joe. "I'll come back another time. I need to talk to my wife. She never seems to be here when I come by and I want to see my girls." He glared at Joe, almost defying him to say something that my dad could find fault with and begin an argument.

"Suit yourself," Joe said, opening the door with his key and disappearing inside.

"You tell your mother I was here and that I want to talk to her. We need to get a lot of things straight." He paused, looking down at me. "How come this guy's got a key to my house?"

"He comes over a lot when my mom isn't home. He does a lot of work around the house. He's very handy." Unlike you, I wanted to add, but I didn't want to get my dad any more riled up than he already was.

My dad's old car was parked in the driveway and he turned and stomped toward it. Before getting inside, he yelled over to me, "I don't know who that guy thinks he is? That's my house he just entered like he owns it. Your mom and I really need to get some things straightened out and the sooner the better."

I shook my head as I watched him drive away. There was something awfully pathetic about my dad. It was obvious to me that he wasn't half the man Joe was. And yet how could I even think that? My dad hadn't killed anybody as far as I knew. Whatever happened to loyalty to one's own family? I wondered, feeling suddenly guilty about how I felt about my own father.

Mom and my sisters returned about an hour later. They looked happy after having a good time together

Dad didn't show up for a week after that. So much for his missing his little girls. I was in my room when the doorbell rang and was hoping against hope that it wasn't him. I knew it wasn't Joe because Joe would have just knocked and come in.

I came out of my room in time to see Mom open the door and my dad step inside. I wanted to be there to give my mom as much support as possible. Leaving her on her own to face my dad did not sit well with me. He was a bully and I knew from my previous conversations with him that he fully intended to try to intimidate my mom. She needed all the support I could give her even if I was only fifteen.

"We need to talk," I heard him say to my mom. He approached my sisters, who stood staring at him like he was an intruder. He picked Sara up and gave her a hug. "Well, how are you making out? Is your mother treating you good?" Sara looked about as uncomfortable as I had ever seen her. Angela was a little too big to be picked up so my dad just gave her a hug.

"It's nice to be back in my own home again," he finally said, looking at my mom. She glared back at him and shook her head.

"I'm afraid this isn't your home any more, John. You've been gone over three years. Did you really think you could just walk in and take over as though you had been gone a few days? We've moved on as a family thinking you were never coming back again."

Dad laughed, but it wasn't a friendly laugh. "Yeah, I can see that. And you've traded me in for another guy. Nice gesture. I'm still your husband you know. And I still own this house."

We were all standing at the entrance looking very uncomfortable. Mom hadn't invited my dad into the living room to sit down. It was quite apparent she didn't want him occupying any more space in our house than was necessary.

"I think you gave up ownership of this house when you left and didn't come back for three years. I've been paying the mortgage and doing the upkeep on our place. What were you doing all that time?"

"That's none of your business. The important thing is, I'm back and I intend to stay back and I intend to live in my own house."

My mom laughed. "That's not going to happen so you can forget that. We have been a happy family since you left. A lot of things have changed. You don't even know your own children. If you intend to stay in town, you can visit the kids whenever you want, but as far as living here again, that's out of the question."

I was really proud of my mom standing up to my dad like that. She was a lot tougher than I had given her credit for.

"Can't we sit down somewhere and talk about this?" my dad asked. He suddenly seemed a lot less confrontational, probably hoping to soften my mom up so she would give in to him.

"No, we can't. There's nothing to discuss. If you want to see the children, you'll have to phone and make arrangements. I'm not sure they'll want to go anywhere with you though, but that's up to them. Now, I would like you to leave. I have people coming over soon and I don't want you being here when they come."

That was news to me, but I guess it was Mom's way of getting rid of my dad. As far as suggesting he could visit us, I think Mom knew that my dad probably wouldn't be bothered doing that. His preference was hanging out with his buddies down at the pub.

He stood uncertainly, looking at the four of us. It was almost like it was us against him. He didn't stand a chance.

Finally, he turned and opened the door. "I'll be back after I see my lawyer," he announced. "And it won't be pretty."

We all went to the door and watched him get into his old car and back recklessly onto the street, almost hitting another car. If the driver of the other car hadn't been alert and slammed on his brakes, there would have been an accident for sure.

We all went into the living room and sat down. Angela put her arm around Mom and gave her a hug. "It's going to be okay," she said. "He's gone and I hope he never comes back."

"Me too," Sara said. "He's mean."

"Well, he's still your father," Mom said. "Even if he isn't much of one."

"I'm not going anywhere with him if he comes over again," Angela announced. "How much fun would that be? I don't even know him any more and he seems really angry."

"Well, knowing your father, I doubt if he'll even make the effort to visit you," Mom said. "But even if he does, you don't have to go with him. I'm sure he can't force you to do anything you don't want to do."

I sat looking at my mom and my sisters and have never been prouder of my family. It was so encouraging how loyal they were and how much of a family we had become without my dad. I didn't want anything to do with him just like my sisters. But I wasn't so sure that getting rid of him was going to be that easy. My dad had a mean streak running right down the middle of his back and he was determined to cause trouble as far as I could see. It was just a matter of us sticking together and not allowing him to have his way. And that might be harder than we thought.

CHAPTER TEN

In the following days there was a tenseness in our house probably because we all were afraid that our dad might show up at any time. Mom took some time off work so that she could be home when we got back from school afraid that Dad might come by when she wasn't there and try to influence us into letting him into the house so that he could worm his way into our lives again. She had a locksmith come by and change all the locks on our doors just in case my dad had a key.

Joe came by frequently so that he could be of assistance in case my dad came by and also to take me for our usual outing. He told me that just because my dad had returned, didn't mean that our visits should change. We visited the boat club where he had his new boat launched and one day he took me out for a short sailing on the lake. I had never been on a boat before so it was quite a thrilling trip for me. The odd thing about it was that we sailed right near where my fort had once been which reminded me that I might be enjoying myself in the company of a murderer. I wasn't sure how to come to terms with that. As time went on, I kept hoping that I had been wrong about Joe and the person I had seen that day wasn't him at all. I began thinking this way because Joe seemed like such a nice guy and with each outing, we became more and more friendly. Our relationship was becoming more like a father-son situation.

When I compared how I was beginning to feel about Joe with my contacts with my dad, I had to shake my head. Joe treated me like a father should treat his son and was always considerate of my feelings. And when we talked, he always listened and took what I said seriously. I could scarcely ever remember having any kind of conversation with my dad when he was at home. He ignored me and my sisters as though we didn't exist. Now that he had returned, he suddenly seemed interested in us which I took with a grain of salt. I was old enough to realize that his sudden interest in his children was just his way of trying to influence my mom into letting him back into our lives.

I still had to come to terms about the Joe problem. I wrestled with that dilemma especially at night before I went to sleep. Now that I knew what kind of person he was and how much time he was willing to spend with me, I could scarcely believe that he had murdered anybody. What a contrast there was between my dad and Joe. I knew my dad wasn't a murderer and yet he treated his whole family badly, while Joe could possibly be a murderer and treated us all with kindness and respect. It was hard to come to terms with the contrast. And with Mom's reminder that appearances could be misleading thrown into the mix, this made my dilemma all the more difficult.

It was good to have my friend Arnie to talk to even though he was sometimes a little cynical and made jokes about my family situation and especially about my dad. Arnie is a very smart guy and once he became serious, he helped me put things into perspective. He was somebody I could bounce things off without being judgmental. We often had lunch together at school in the cafeteria and the topic invariably got around to what was happening about my dad.

"Has your old man been around hassling you guys lately?" he wanted to know.

I shook my head. "He's been keeping a pretty low profile. I'm a little surprised he hasn't shown up, but considering the situation, maybe that isn't so surprising. But I can't help wondering what he's up to. He seemed pretty determined to weasel his way back into our lives the last time we talked to him. But to be honest, I'm relieved he's stayed away. I keep hoping maybe he'll give up and leave us alone for good."

Arnie laughed. "That might be a little bit of wishful thinking. Or more likely a whole lot of wishful thinking. I don't think your dad has any thought of giving up on you guys. After all, you're living in his house for one thing. That must really gall him. And then there's our guy Joe. I can just imagine what he's thinking about some guy horning in on his wife and in his own house. What a conundrum. That would be enough to drive any guy insane let alone a guy like your dad who's already half way there."

If there was one thing about Arnie, he could be really blunt once he got going. For a sixteen-year-old (he was a year older than me) he was quite perceptive though. And he didn't care what people thought about him when he said outrageous things. I must admit, I envied that side of his personality, probably because I was just the opposite.

"Any thoughts about what I should do about Joe?" I asked him. I really needed some advice as I had run out of options and was feeling guilty about beginning to really like Joe.

He shook his head. "Short of asking him if he has ever killed anybody, I can't think of anything. I'm getting the feeling you're really beginning to like this guy. Right? Well, if I were you, I would just go with the flow as my dad always says. Don't make waves and enjoy his company. Sometimes killers can be really nice guys." He laughed and punched me on the shoulder

"I don't know any killers so I don't know if some of them are nice guys. I suppose it's logical that some of them are, just by the law of averages."

"The law of averages tells me that you're dead wrong about thinking you saw Joe that day. So, as far as I'm concerned, you're burning yourself out and losing sleep over nothing. You would be better off spending your time thinking about Arla Vanderwall who sits right next to you in math. She's a fox to end all foxes, so how come you haven't made a move on her?"

Sometimes Arnie can throw me a curve right in the middle of a serious conversation. "Arla Vanderwall! Are you kidding? She wouldn't give me the time of day if I was the last guy on earth. Besides, she's already got a boyfriend and he's a lot bigger than I am."

"Yeah, well I heard from a reliable source that she's got the hots for you."

"Oh really? And who did you hear that from?" I was beginning to get excited, but knowing Arnie, he was probably blowing hot air. Then again, if he wasn't, this little rumor needed looking into.

"I never name my sources," Arnie exclaimed, "otherwise I would never be privy to some of the hottest gossip in the school. You gotta respect your sources and be able to keep your mouth shut." He leered over at me. "So, what are you going to do about it, lover boy?"

I shook my head. As if I didn't already have enough on my plate without thinking about whether Arla had the hots for me. If she did, and that seemed about as likely as me winning a million-dollar lottery, I was flattered-more than flattered. I was flabbergasted. Unfortunately, I wasn't in a position to do anything about it. For one thing I was far too timid to just walk up to her say, "Hi toots, wanna go to a movie?" That just wasn't me, worst luck. Furthermore, as far as I could see, Arla had never even looked at me or spoken to me the whole year. Now did that seem like a girl who has the hots for me? Nada.

"What I'm going to do about it is..." I was looking at Arnie and he was looking back at me literally hanging on the edge in anticipation. He liked the unexpected, the mysterious, but I wasn't about to give it to him. "I really hate to disappoint Arla, but, well, what can I say, Arnie? She just isn't my type."

"Not your type?" he almost screamed. "She's everybody's type. She's got the whole darn school, at least all the guys, on tether hooks. This is one foxy gal. Have you lost your mind?"

"Well, you could take her out," I countered.

"No, no, no. She hasn't got the hots for me. It's you she's after, you and only you and you've got to do something about it or else I'm going to go stark raving mad."

I'd forgotten about Arnie's dramatic side. He could get excited about the most ridiculous things. After I had calmed him down and assured him that I would make my move soon, he rewarded me with a wide grin.

"Now you're talking like a good old, red-blooded American boy. I'm very pleased with you. I expect you to keep me updated on your progress."

I did promise him, but I had no intentions of keeping it. Arnie had very subtly distracted me from my other problems. Very sneaky of him. Arla was going to have to be put on the back burner and I was going to have to be very inventive concerning my progress in wooing her if I was going to convince Arnie. Then again maybe a smile now and again and a "hi, how are you?" wouldn't hurt just in case what Arnie told me was true.

I chuckled all the way home about how excited Arnie had got. You would have thought he had some stake in my unlikely liaison with Arla. Maybe a vicarious thrill was what turned him on.

I suddenly forgot all about our crazy conversation in the cafeteria when I saw my dad's old car parked out in front of our house. He hadn't shown his face for over two weeks and I was beginning to think that maybe he had given up on us. Now, here he was again like a bad omen. As I got closer on my bike, I could see him sitting in his car smoking a cigarette. He rolled down his window when I drew up beside his car.

"How you doing, kid? I came over to talk to your ma, but nobody's answering the door. I know somebody's in there because I saw the curtains move."

"She doesn't want to talk to you," I told him.

"Well, I want to talk to her. We've got a lot to talk about. I got rights here. I still own that house she's living in. And I want to see my girls. I'm sure they miss their old dad."

"No, they don't," I assured him. "They're afraid of you."

"That's because they haven't seen me for awhile. Once I talk to them, they'll come around. Every little girl needs a dad. They're no different."

I had to laugh at that. My dad was living in a dream world if he thought he was going to win my sisters over. They were pretty stubborn and had a mind of their own. They definitely took after my dad. And I, thankfully, took after my mom.

I left him sitting in his car and pedalled up our driveway, put away my bike and went into the house. My mom and two sisters were sitting in the living room looking like three hostages. They looked genuinely afraid.

"Did you talk to him?" Mom wanted to know.

I nodded. "Same old story. He wants his house back and he wants to talk to Sara and Angela."

"I'm not talking to him," Angela said. "I don't want anything to do with him." She turned to her mother. "I don't have to, do I Mom?"

"Of course not, dear. I phoned Joe. He's coming over. That should dissuade your dad from coming into the house."

"If only he would just go away for good," Angela said, looking at my mom. "He gives me the creeps."

Ten minutes later, Joe pulled into the driveway. We watched from the front window as he strolled out to Dad's car and spoke to my dad. Whatever they said to one another, it was of short duration. Dad's car pulled away and we all breathed a sigh of relief.

"He said he'll be back," Joe said when he had entered the front door. He came over and sat down beside my mom and put his arm around her. "What a nuisance. I hope he didn't scare you guys too much."

"I'm not sure what to do about him," my mom said. "It's not as though I can get a restraining order or anything. After all, this is his house and these are his children. I don't think a judge would approve of what we're doing. He's probably got every right to see his kids."

"I think he gave up a lot of his rights when he left for three years. Surely that must mean something," Joe said.

I felt a little trapped, caught between a hostile dad and a possible murderer. What was I supposed to do? Maybe a duel between the two of them would solve half the problem. The trouble was, I wasn't even sure who I hoped would survive the duel.

CHAPTER ELEVEN

Our lives continued as it always had just as though my dad didn't exist. But the thought that he might show up again was always in the back of our minds. Joe and mom seemed to be getting along better and better as the days progressed. I didn't have to worry about mom suddenly telling us that they were going to get married because she was already married. I definitely didn't want her marrying a killer or at least a possible killer. I felt it was up to me to find out the truth about Joe. But I had no idea how to go about that. I had already searched amongst the trees at the beach and found nothing. That didn't make much sense to me. If a body was buried in there, you would think there would be some sign of it, but there wasn't. Despite it being over three years ago, there should still be something there to indicate a grave.

I went back there a time or two and even contemplated going into the trees and looking again, but I didn't do that. I'm not sure why. Maybe I was afraid I might actually find a grave. To be honest, I was hoping that Joe was innocent, that he was just what he said he was, a teacher and a volunteer and nothing more.

When I told Arnie that I was still worried about Joe, he looked at me and shook his head. We were sitting out in front of the school watching the cheerleaders go through their routine.

"You've got a real monkey on your back, haven't you? I hope you get rid of him before your old age. I can't even imagine how it must feel sitting around worrying whether your mom's boyfriend is a murderer or just a nice innocent guy."

"It isn't pleasant," I told him. "And it's wearing me down. Sometimes I think I'm about to go bonkers. If there was only a fairy flying around who would grant me my every wish. I know what I would be asking her."

"You're a basket case all right," Arnie conceded. "You need professional help and I'm the guy who can put you on the road to recovery."

"And just how would you be doing that?"

Arnie heaved a big sigh. "We have to look at this whole problem from a practical point of view. First of all, did you actually see Joe commit a murder? The answer is no. Did you actually see him carry a woman into the trees? The answer is yes and no. Yes, you saw somebody carry a woman into the trees, but was it really Joe? Probably not. If this scenario actually existed, from a logical point of view, there should be some sign of where he actually buried the woman. Right?"

"Right," I said. "But I've been all over that area and there's no sign that somebody's buried there."

"Then, using logic, what you saw wasn't what you thought it was, or there actually is some kind of grave or mound or indication that a body was buried there. You just didn't find it. Right?"

"Right. Except I looked pretty thoroughly."

Arnie looked thoughtful. "Okay, but remember, you were only twelve at the time. The twelve-year-old brain isn't exactly fully formed. You might have been mistaken about exactly where this woman was buried."

I had to concede that he could well be correct. "So, what's the answer? What do we do?"

Arnie chuckled and gave me a shrewd look. "We do what is logical. We go out there and start looking in earnest. If that grave is there, we should be able to find it. A quick run through won't work. We've got to search every square inch of that area. And if we do, I'm almost positive we'll be rewarded. Give me five."

I held up my hand and he gave it a resounding slap. Maybe, just maybe he was onto something.

"You would do that for me?" I asked.

"Hey, what are friends for? Besides, I hate seeing you dragging yourself around as though the world is about to come to an end. I want the old Ryan Sinclair back again. However, there is one proviso."

"What might that be? That I give you my first- born child?"

"Nothing so sinister," Arnie said. "We're not dealing with a fairy tale here, but actual reality."

Arnie was enjoying keeping me in suspense.

"You have to promise me that you'll make a move on Arla. That's all I ask. What could be simpler?"

Somehow, in the back of my mind, I knew there was going to be a price for all this, but as I thought about it, it didn't seem all that onerous. In fact, it might prove to be quite rewarding.

"Okay, I'll do it. But if we don't find anything out there, then the bets off. Right?"

"Right but look at this whole thing in a positive way. If we find evidence of a grave and then you have to make a move on Arla, wow! Your life is going to undergo a one-eighty- degree change that should just about bring you back to the way you used to be. I'm counting on that."

"What if Arla laughs in my face. Then what?"

"There you go being negative again. Like I told you before, I have it from a good source that she's after your bod. You haven't got a thing to worry about."

Right after school, we pedalled out to the beach. We had at least two hours before we had to be home. That should be enough time to find what we were looking for.

We put our bikes down on the spot directly facing where my fort had once been and stood looking around. "Where do we start?" I asked.

Arnie was busily looking out over the lake enjoying the light breeze that lifted his hair and made him look a little like a scarecrow. I chuckled inwardly at the thought. His ears stuck out and with his hair flying around, he looked quite comical.

He turned and looked up the treeline. "Let's start way up there," he pointed. "I'm thinking you've probably covered the area around your fort pretty well. You don't know how far into the trees he might have carried his quarry."

So, we walked about a hundred yards up from my fort and then entered the trees. It was dense in there and walking around wasn't easy. Somehow, I couldn't imagine anybody carrying a body and trying to find a suitable place to bury it.

After about a half-an-hour, I was beginning to lose hope. We hadn't discovered anything resembling a grave or a mound where somebody was buried. I looked over at Arnie, but he didn't seem to be deterred at all. In fact, he looked quite sure that we were going to find *something*. I was beginning to wish that I had his optimism.

Ten minutes later we found it. Or at least what we thought might be it. Over time the hole that the killer had dug sunk and was now clearly outlined. It looked to be about six feet long and three feet wide. We both sat down on a log and looked at each other. "Well, what do you think?" Arnie asked. "Does that look like a grave or what?"

It looked like a grave all right, but I wasn't about to go scrounging around and digging it up. I had never seen a dead body, at least one up close up, and I wasn't about to start.

"It looks like one," I said. "Now what do we do?"

"We definitely don't start digging it up. We might find more than we bargained for. Besides, if there really is a dead body under there, I don't think the cops would be impressed if we messed up a crime scene."

We both stood there looking down at the site as though it contained the secret of the ages.

"It's no wonder I couldn't find it," I finally said. "It's fifty yards away from where I thought it might be."

We eventually went back to our bikes and pedalled back into town. After saying so-long to Arnie and assuring him that I would look after things, I reached home still wondering what I should do. I knew I would have to tell the cops and leave it with them whether they believed me or not. But should I tell my mom? Especially since I suspected Joe was the perpetrator and Mom was sure to tell him what I had discovered.

"Well, you're a little late," Mom said when I entered the house. "Somebody keep you after school?"

"No. Arnie and I went for a little ride down to the beach," I said offhandedly.

"Supper won't be long," she said.

I went to my room and lay down on my bed, staring up at the ceiling. Now that I had concrete proof that there was a dead body out there amongst the trees, I suddenly felt like an even heavier load was on my shoulders. I couldn't just ignore it. That would drive me crazy for sure. I definitely had to go and tell the cops what I knew. And if they didn't believe me, that was their problem, not mine.

Carrying a secret around in my head for the next twenty-four hours wasn't going to be easy. I had decided not to tell my mom. Why burden her with what I knew. She would just be upset and want to know every little detail. I could hardly tell her who I suspected killed that person buried at the beach. That would send my mom into orbit. I was just going to have to tell the cops and see where things went from there. Maybe, at last, I would have an answer to the riddle that had been driving me crazy for the last three years.

The next day after school, I went down to the cop shop. I knew exactly where it was because I had passed it many times on my way to the beach.

When I got to the entrance, I paused, having second thoughts about what I was about to do, but after taking a deep breath, I entered, resolved to get this mystery solved and get my life back.

The man at the desk waved me over after I sat down on a bench just inside the door.

"What can I do for you, young man?" he asked.

"I want to report a crime," I said. I could barely get the words out of my mouth, I was so nervous.

"A crime?" he said. "What kind of a crime?"

"A murder." There, it was out and I could start breathing again. The cop behind the desk looked at me as though I had two heads.

"That's a pretty serious crime," he finally said. "Maybe you had better tell me about it."

I did my best to explain everything I knew about the murder. Of course, I didn't tell him who I suspected the murderer was. After all, I could be mistaken and all hell would break loose if my accusation ever got back to Mom and Joe.

The cop stared at me for several seconds as though trying to make up his mind whether I was on the level or not.

"You were only twelve when you witnessed this?" he asked. "How old are you now?"

"Fifteen," I told him. "It's been bothering me for a long time."

"Why didn't you come in and report this at the time?"

I was afraid he was going to ask that and I didn't really have an answer except that it was hard for me to believe that what I had seen was actually a murder. It took a while for it to dawn on me.

"I don't know. I guess I was afraid."

"I can understand that," he said kindly. "After all, you were only twelve. Right?"

"Right," I said. He stood up and came around his desk and approached me. He held out his hand. "I'm Corporal Larson. We appreciate you coming in and reporting this. We depend on people like you to let us know when you see a crime."

I shook his hand. He seemed quite old to be a cop, but I liked him right away.

"I'm just going to go and talk to one of the detectives. I'll be right back."

He disappeared down a long hallway and entered a room. A few minutes later, he came out followed by a much younger man.

"This is detective Evans," he told me when the two men came up to me. Detective Evans held out his hand and I shook it.

"I'm Ryan Sinclair," I told him. He smiled at me and then looked over at Corporal Larson. I was almost sure that he winked at Corporal Larson, but I wasn't sure.

"Why don't you follow me and we'll find a room where we can have a little chat," Detective Evans said.

After trying a few doors, he finally found a room that was open and unoccupied.

"Have a seat," he said, gesturing toward a chair that had several books on it. He came over and took the books and placed them on a desk and then sat down.

"You've dropped quite a little bombshell here this afternoon," he said, looking over at me and giving me the onceover. "Maybe you had better explain exactly what you saw way back then."

I told him what I had told Corporal Larson and again without mentioning that I thought Joe was the culprit. He listened carefully and nodded several times. When I had finished, he smiled at me.

"That's quite a story. It must have been pretty scary for you at the time."

I shook my head. "Not really. I didn't exactly realize what was happening right in front of me. It wasn't until later that it began to sink in. It was kind of like a delayed reaction I guess."

"Well, what we need to do now is go out to where you discovered the gravesite and have a look. Are you up to that?"

"Yes sir. No problem."

"Okay." He smiled at me. "I'm just going to go and pick up a shovel. I'll be back in a moment."

I felt excited and yet I had no desire to see a dead body. If a dead body was found, it would confirm what I had seen that day and that would give me a certain amount of satisfaction. Nobody could say that it was all in my imagination or that I had been seeing things that really didn't exist.

Detective Evans reappeared carrying a shovel and we went out to his patrol car. On the way back to the beach, he asked me some questions about where I went to school and what some of my interests were. He seemed quite interested in finding out about me. He told me that he had gone to the very school I was now attending and I was surprised when he named some of the teachers that were still teaching at my school.

By the time we arrived at the beach, I felt quite relaxed about what I was facing. The thought that what we had discovered might not be a gravesite at all didn't even occur to me.

After taking the shovel out of the trunk of his car, we headed into the trees where Arnie and I had discovered what looked like a gravesite. It took me a little while to find it again because it was so dense and dark in there. Everywhere I turned looked the same, but I eventually found the grave.

We both stood there looking at what had once been a hole and I suddenly didn't feel quite as confident as I had previously felt. It was going to be embarrassing if there wasn't a body under there. I wondered what Detective Evans' reaction would be. Would he be angry at me? Shake his head and tell me what a dope I was leading him on a wild goose chase? I hoped not.

"It might be a good idea for you to go back to my car and wait for me. I'm pretty sure you don't want to see what might be under here. Right?"

"Right," I said.

"I shouldn't be long."

I made my way back through the trees and sat down on the sand beside his car. I tried not to think about anything, but my mind kept going back to that day when I was twelve and seeing that man carrying the woman. Now that I thought about it, it was quite a frightening scene. I guess because I was only twelve and pretty naïve, I was protected from becoming too alarmed.

About ten minutes later, Detective Evans appeared carrying the shovel. Without saying anything, he opened the trunk and threw the shovel inside. Then he turned to me.

"There's a body there all right, Ryan." He turned away and looked out across the water. He just stood there with his back to me without saying anything for several minutes. I wasn't sure what he was doing. Maybe he was upset about what he saw.

He finally turned and looked over at me. "Well, let's go back to the station. This place is going to be a crime scene so don't come back here until the investigation is over. Okay?"

"Okay," I said. I wasn't sure how I felt. On the one hand I was kind of glad that what Arnie and I had discovered would help the police and maybe a murder mystery would be solved because of us. On the other hand, it was kind of gruesome, that somebody (I still hoped it wasn't Joe) had committed a murder and buried their body here. It was quite upsetting.

We went back to the police station. Detective Evans shook my hand. "We appreciate what you've done, Ryan. You're a brave young man. Now, I want you to go home and not even think about this for awhile, if that's possible. We'll be in contact with you in a few days. We'd like to talk to your parents and your friend Arnie."

I pedalled home as fast as I could, doing my best to put this whole episode out of my mind, but I wasn't being very successful. I knew I would have to tell Mom what had taken place. I wondered what her reaction might be. She had been pretty skeptical when I had told her about this over three years ago.

"Where have you been?" she wanted to know as soon as I entered the house. "I've been a little worried about you."

"I need to talk to you, Mom. It's real important."

She led me over to the couch and we sat down beside one another. "Are you in trouble?" she wanted to know. She looked about as serious as I've ever seen her. "Did something happen at school?"

I shook my head. "No." I wasn't even sure how to begin. I didn't want to scare my mom. She already looked upset and I didn't want her to worry unnecessarily.

"Arnie and I found a grave out at the beach. Remember when I told you about seeing a man carrying a woman into the trees there?" My mom nodded, looking more and more concerned. "Well, Detective Evans and I went out there today and he discovered a body."

"Oh my gosh, Ryan. I can hardly believe that. How are you feeling? It must be awful for you."

"I'm okay. I didn't see the body or anything."

"So, you told the police about seeing a man carry a woman into the trees and then you and this detective went out there? Is that right?"

I nodded. "Arnie and I went out there yesterday and found the grave. That's when I knew I had to tell the cops."

Mom put her arms around me and held me for several seconds. When she released me, I could see tears running down her face. "I'm so sorry I didn't take you more seriously," she said, wiping away the tears. "And all this time, you were worrying about what was out there. I don't know why I didn't take the whole thing more seriously. You were only twelve then, weren't you? I should have questioned you more about what you saw. We could have gone to the police and maybe they would have looked into a possible murder. Oh, Ryan, I feel terrible, like I let you down."

"It's okay, Mom. At least now the cops might be able to solve a murder." They also might discover that Joe was the killer. I hoped that that was never going to happen. Mom and Joe had become such good friends and he had become such an important part of our family, I didn't want him to be guilty. My mom would be devastated if that ever happened.

The next day at school, I told Arnie all about my little trip out to the beach with Detective Evans and him finding a body.

"Wow! This is turning into a real mystery," he said. "And here we are right in the middle of it. I'd say that's pretty exciting."

"I wish all this wasn't happening. It's upsetting, especially to my mom. I would like to get my life back, have everything back to normal."

"Hey, consider it an adventure. It's not every day that you're responsible for helping to solve a murder. Maybe they'll make a movie out of this some day and you and I'll be front and centre. Pretty nifty I would say."

"The cops are going to want to talk to you," I said. "Since you were part of finding the grave and all that."

"I don't mind. I'm not sure what I can tell them, but being in the middle of all this makes me feel a little like a celebrity. Maybe we'll get our picture in the paper and get interviewed by a reporter."

"I don't think that will happen since we're minors, and to be honest, I would just as soon remain anonymous."

Arnie laughed. "You're much too modest my friend. When you're a hero, you have to step up and accept the accolades."

"Hero? I don't think I'm a hero at all. I just happened to see something that I wish I hadn't seen. My life would be much simpler and my mom wouldn't be upset."

After school, I pedalled home only to find Joe's truck parked in the driveway. Joe was the last person I wanted to see at this point, but at least it would give me the opportunity to study his reaction to what had been going on. I was sure Mom had told him all about what had happened yesterday.

My two sisters were sitting beside Joe in the living room when I entered. I was surprised that one of them wasn't in his lap and the other hanging onto his neck, they were so taken with him. Nice for Mom I guess that her girls were so enthusiastic about her boyfriend.

"Hey, young man, you're becoming quite the gumshoe," Joe said, as I sat across from him. "Nice going. Your Mom told me all about it."

"What's a gumshoe?" Sara wanted to know.

Looking disgusted, Angela said, "it's a detective, silly. Don't you know anything?"

I looked at Joe. He looked like the Joe I saw almost every day. The discovery of the body didn't seem to be having much effect on him. Either that, or he was an awfully good actor.

My mom appeared from the kitchen still looking concerned and probably worried that her little boy was traumatized and about to go off the deep end. I didn't feel anything like that. I was more interested in Joe's reaction than anything else. If he was guilty, surely, he would show some indication of that.

"I explained everything to Joe," Mom said. "I thought he should know. I hope you don't mind me telling him."

"No...no, not at all," I managed.

"How does it feel to be in the middle of murder case?" Joe asked. "I sure never had anything like that happen to me when I was your age." I shrugged. "Pretty awesome, I guess." I didn't feel like it was awesome at all. I just wanted it to go away. And I wanted to find out in the worst way whether Joe had any part in it.

"Well, I hope they find the culprit who committed the murder," my mom said. "And the sooner the better. I'm sure we'll all sleep better when he's brought to justice."

I said a silent amen to that.

"The fact that the body has been lying out there for the last three years is going to make it difficult to solve the case," Joe said. "But not impossible, of course." He looked at my sisters. "I guess we shouldn't be talking about this in front of you girls."

"I can take it," Angela said. "But I don't know about my pip-squeak of a sister. She's a bit of a sissy."

This caused Sara to stick her tongue out at Angela.

"Whoever did this must be a monster," Mom said. "Imagine killing someone and then burying them in a shallow grave. Awful."

"They're probably a psychopath," I said, looking at Joe. "No feelings of guilt, no conscience."

Joe looked interested. "So, what do you know about psychopaths? That's not something most fifteen- year- old's know anything about."

I gave him my best nonchalant look. "I read about them in a book I found in the library. It was very informative." The thought occurred to me that if Joe was the man I had seen carrying the woman into the trees, then he could well be a psychopath. And I couldn't even warn my mom without causing a flurry and making my mom even more upset than she already was.

CHAPTER TWELVE

Two days later, Detective Evans phoned me and asked me to come down to the police station and bring Arnie with me. I told him I couldn't come down until after school and he said he would be in his office all day. He also wanted my mom there since we were underaged. Mom agreed to meet us at the police station at four o'clock.

Arnie was all smiles when I told him about the phone call. He loved to be in the middle of things like this. "It gives my dull life a little flavor," he said. "I've been a mystery fan all my life and here I am, right in the middle of one. What more could one ask?"

I rolled my eyes. I didn't want to be in the middle of anything right now. All I wanted was for all of this to go away. I wanted peace and quiet and serenity in my life. Was that so much to ask?

After school, Arnie and I pedalled down to the cop shop to meet with Detective Evans. Arnie talked non-stop all the way there. You would have thought we were going to a rock concert or something thrilling like that instead being interrogated by a detective. This was definitely not something I was looking forward to.

"Nice to see you again, Ryan," Detective Evans said. He turned to Arnie. "You must be Arnie, right?" He held out his hand and Arnie shook it. "Nice to meet you."

Arnie was all smiles. "Quite a murder case you got going here," he said. "Any developments yet?"

"I'm afraid not, but it's early. And the fact that we have a body is going to help a lot thanks to you boys."

We followed Detective Evans down the hallway and into a small office where my mom was sitting in a chair looking at a magazine. She didn't look comfortable as though she would have preferred being anywhere else than the police station. Arnie's mom sat across from her. The two moms didn't know each other very well, but they seemed to be getting along just fine considering the circumstances.

"Hi dear," Mom said, when I appeared at the door. When she saw Arnie, she managed a smile. My mom really likes Arnie and always said that he was the smartest sixteen-year-old she knew. "How are you, Arnie? Everything going okay?"

"About as good as it can get," Arnie said, sitting down on a chair beside his mom and giving my mom his best smile that he always seemed to be able to turn on at any given moment.

Detective Evans sat down at his desk and pulled out a writing pad from a drawer. "First of all, I want to thank you boys for what you've done—finding that grave and then coming down here and reporting it. You have certainly done your civic duty and assisted us in solving this case. Let me compliment you, Mrs. Sinclair, in bringing up such a fine boy as Ryan." He looked at Arnie's mom. "The same goes for you and Arnie, Mrs. Weeks. We thank you as well for the assistance you've both given us."

My mom smiled over at me. She looked proud, but I was worried about her. Little did she know that her boyfriend might be the psychopath we had talked about last night. I had hoped that Joe would give himself away when we discussed the murder, but other than looking concerned, he didn't show any signs of guilt. Now, here was the detective about to investigate the crime and I couldn't tell him anything about Joe with Mom sitting right there for one thing, and for another, I wasn't even sure he was the killer.

"There are a number of things I would like to ask you," Detective Evans said, looking at me and then at Arnie. "First off, can you describe the man who you saw carry the woman into the trees?"

Oh boy, this was all I needed. I guess I could tell him that he looked exactly like Joe, my Mom's boyfriend, but I wasn't about to do that. "He was tall and thin and had sandy hair and a moustache," I told him. I looked over at Mom hoping she wouldn't put two and two together and realize that the killer was a lot like Joe.

"How old would you say he was? As close as you can guess."

I had no real clue how old Joe was, but I figured he was around my mom's age and she was forty something. "About the same age as my mom I think. I'm not very good at figuring out the ages of adults."

Detective Evans laughed. "I can understand that," he said.

Over the next hour, Detective Evans asked us a whole lot of questions, most of which I couldn't answer.

Before we left, Detective Evans shook hands with us again. "We'll keep you informed of any developments," he said, looking at Mom and Mrs. Weeks. "Since this is now a three-year-old case, it's going to be a little harder to solve, but I'm sure we'll find whoever was responsible eventually."

As we pedalled home, Arnie seemed even more excited than he was before we arrived at the police station. "Man, I sure hope they find the guy," he said. "A lot of people are going to be nervous with a guy like that walking around." He laughed. "I think you can relax about your mom's boyfriend. The more I think about that, the more I'm convinced it isn't him. You need to relax too old chap. You're far too uptight."

Arnie was right on that score. I was uptight. The sooner all this stuff was cleared up and the killer brought to justice, whether it was Joe or somebody else, the happier I would be.

Not only did I have to worry about whether Joe was a murderer, I also had to worry about my dad and what he was doing. We hadn't seen him for quite awhile, but that didn't mean much. Knowing my dad, he would soon be showing up like an unwanted guest, and sure enough, the day after our visit to the cop shop, Dad arrived on our doorstep.

Angela answered the door and immediately called me. I was in my bedroom working on a home assignment. Mom had a medical appointment she couldn't miss. Wouldn't you know Dad would appear on the one day she wasn't with us. So, there we were, having to deal with our dad by ourselves, something I didn't exactly relish.

When I came to the door, Dad was standing inside talking to Angela. Sara was in the living room watching TV obviously not wanting to see her dad.

"Hey Ryan. How are things?" Dad said when I appeared from my bedroom. "Thought I would drop around and see what you kids are up to. I was thinking we might take a little drive, get to know each other again. What do you think?"

I looked at Angela, who was standing behind my dad shaking her head vigorously. I looked at my watch. It was almost five o'clock. "It's kind of late. Mom will be home any minute to make supper. And I'm in the middle of a homework assignment. Maybe another time?"

My dad didn't look happy. "Look, since I've come back I've scarcely had time to talk to you guys. Remember, I'm your dad. Just because I was gone for awhile, doesn't mean I don't care about you or that I'm not your dad any more. Nothing has changed. I would like to talk to my kids, get to know you again. You know, like old times."

I almost laughed out loud. What a load of garbage! He leaves for over three years and now he expects us to just accept him as though nothing has changed? He must be living in an alternate universe. And that crack about "old times". That was a joke. My dad treated me as though I was a stranger, somebody to be ignored, before he disappeared. Now I was supposed to believe he wanted to be like a father figure. Good luck.

"Mom told us not to go anywhere until she came home," I told him. "I think she's having company for supper."

"Ha! I suppose the company is that boyfriend of hers." He shook his head and then smiled when Sara appeared. "Well, how's my little girl?" he said. "Have you missed your dad?"

Sara was the only one of us that my dad made a fuss over before he left. I was a little afraid she might get taken in by him, but she just stared without saying anything.

"You've sure grown. I wouldn't have recognized you. You've turned into a real beautiful young lady."

If he thought flattery was going to work, I had news for him. Sara was pretty immune from that kind of thing.

My dad stood there in the hallway looking at the three of us, not saying anything, probably wondering what he should do next. He couldn't physically remove us from the house and get us into his car. If we didn't want to go with him, there wasn't much he could do.

"Well, I'm really disappointed in you kids," he finally said, turning toward the door. "Here I make the gesture to get to know my family again and I get turned down by my own kids. That's really heartbreaking." He paused before going out the door. "I'm not giving up though. I'll be back. I hope you'll think about your old dad and getting to know me again."

When he had gone, my sisters went back into the living room and I went to my bedroom. I could hardly believe what had just happened. If there was one person I didn't want to deal with it was my dad—especially when my mom wasn't there.

That was the last time I saw my dad for over a month. I ran into him in the mall one Saturday afternoon. He was with some woman. I guess she was his girlfriend. He introduced me, but I wasn't very interested to be honest. He tried to convince her how proud he was of me and what a nice young man I had turned out to be. What a load of garbage. If she believed him, she didn't give any indication of it. I told him I was in a hurry and hightailed it out of there as fast as I could.

Mom and Joe had become a real item and I think he spent more time at our house than he did at his own. All three of us kids really liked him and accepted him as a kind of substitute dad I suppose. I was still caught between two worlds as far as Joe was concerned. We hadn't heard anything from Detective Evans about whether they had solved the case at the beach, so my feelings about Joe were still in limbo. I still clung to the hope that it wasn't him. If he turned out to be guilty, our lives, and especially my mom's, would be completely turned upside down. I desperately didn't want that to happen. I know Mom worried a lot about my dad, about the house and whether Dad would insist on taking possession of it or forcing her to sell it. But so far nothing had happened.

If Joe turned out to be a murderer, I was worried about my mom. Knowing what I knew and not saying anything to her could end up being the worst thing that could ever happen to me. I had told myself a million times that I should tell Mom about Joe, but I could never seem to bring myself to do it. Mom was already on pins and needles concerning my dad and I didn't want to add to her worries.

But did I have an obligation to tell her? I had information that could end up being really important and I was keeping it to myself. Why couldn't I just tell her? It wouldn't be the end of the world and it might end up saving her life or saving her from possibly marrying Joe.

CHAPTER THIRTEEN

Over the next few months, I thought a lot about my dad and when he might show up at our doorstep again, but my biggest worry was about Joe. I thought I was doing pretty well concealing my feelings and acting as though everything was fine in my life, but I guess I was wrong. Mom could see through me like I was a pane of glass.

"I'm worried about you, Ryan," she said one night while we were watching TV. "Are you sleeping all right? You look tired and worn down to me. Something is going on. Are you worried about your dad?"

"No, not at all," I said. "Everything's okay. Really."

She gave me that look and shook her head. She turned off the TV. My sisters had gone to bed and there was just the two of us. "I wasn't born yesterday. I know when something is bothering you. You know you can talk to me about anything, Ryan. I always try not to be judgmental when you tell me things. If you're in trouble I would like to know. Maybe I can help you. After all, I am your mom and what are moms for if not to be a sounding board for her children. Keeping secrets just isn't going to do it."

"I am worried about something," I finally said, "but I can't tell you about it." Oh, why did I say that? Now she'll never leave me alone until she finds out what's bugging me.

There was that look again. The best I can describe it is a pained expression combined with a skepticism that always seemed to get to me. Keeping secrets from my mom was like a case of poison ivy. It wouldn't leave me alone until I dealt with it.

She reached over and put her arm around me. "Out with it young man. You'll feel much better getting it off your conscience. Trust me on that score."

I tried not to look at her, but that was hard with her face almost touching mine. "It's about Joe," I finally said.

"Joe? What about him? I thought you two were getting along great. I thought you really liked him?" When I didn't say anything, she nodded her head. "Oh, I get it. You're worried he's taking up so much of my time that I'm neglecting you, that I love him more than I love you. Is that it?" When I shrugged, she continued: "Darling, you and the girls are the most important people in my life. Just because Joe and I like each other, doesn't mean I love you any less. I've got lots of room to love you all. Can you understand that?"

"That's not it," I finally said.

"Oh! Well, I'm glad about that." She paused, looking a little confused. "So, what is it?"

"That man at the beach who was carrying a lady into the trees—" I stopped, wondering if I could ever get the words out. Mom was looking at me anxiously. Her blue eyes were as round and focussed as I had ever seen them. It was a little scary. "I think it was Joe."

She didn't say anything for several seconds as though she couldn't quite understand what I had just said. "Joe?" she finally said. "I don't understand. Why would you think it was Joe?"

"It looked just like him. I'm almost sure it was him." "Honey, you were only twelve years old at the time. That was over three years ago." She smiled suddenly. "You mean to tell me that you've been carrying this around in your head all this time? Why didn't you say something?"

"I didn't want to hurt you. I know how much you like Joe."

Mom looked at me. She didn't seem to be concerned at all, which worried me a little. Why hadn't what I just told her blown her away?

"Did you tell Detective Evans that you thought Joe was involved?"

I shook my head.

"Well, I'm glad of that." She smiled at me and kissed me on the top of my head. "You realise that it probably wasn't Joe, just somebody who looks like him. You were only twelve. At that age a lot of adults look alike."

"I guess so." The fact that my mom wasn't upset was a big relief to me. And unloading about Joe—well, that was a relief too, even though I still wondered if it could have been him.

"Now, aren't you glad we had this little talk?" Mom said. "And don't you even think that Joe could do such a thing. He's a wonderful person and I don't for a minute think he's capable of killing anyone and burying them like that." She gave me a big hug. "Thanks for telling me everything. It must have been hard for you."

"Please don't tell him anything about what I told you. He would probably not want to talk to me ever again if he knew."

"Of course, I won't. Your secret is safe with me. But even if I did, I'm sure Joe would understand."

I slept better that night having gotten what I had seen at the beach off my mind. What was even better, Mom wasn't upset and seemed convinced that whoever I had seen, it wasn't Joe, just somebody who looked like him. I hoped she was right. If I was wrong, somewhere out there, Joe had a twin.

CHAPTER FOURTEEN

About two weeks later, I got a phone call from Detective Evans. He wanted my mom and I to come down to the station as soon as we could. I was desperate to ask him if they had found the person who had murdered that girl, but he had hung up before I had a chance.

When Mom got home, I told her about Detective Evans's call and that we had to go straight down to the police station. I was excited that at last they had nabbed the person responsible for a murder and that I had had a hand in bringing the person to justice. Of course, I was hoping that whoever the culprit was, that it wasn't Joe.

Detective Evans smiled at me as he came up the hallway where Mom and I were sitting waiting for his appearance. Whether that was a good sign or not, I wasn't sure.

"Come on down to my office," he said, shaking my hand and leading us back down the hallway. He sat behind his desk and looked over at us. Both Mom and I must have looked like two curious birds.

"Well, first of all, I have good news. We have arrested a man we suspect committed the murder at the beach. Of course, he denies it, but from the evidence we have, it looks like a pretty open and shut case. I got you down here, because I wanted you to take a look at a group of photographs and tell me whether you recognize any of them. Do you think you could do that?" When I nodded, he continued. "That's great. I know it's been a long time since you witnessed what took place out there, but if you can positively identify the man you saw, that would help our case enormously."

He reached into a file he had on his desk and took out six photographs and laid them out in front of me. I took a deep breath and looked at them. It didn't take me long to identify the man I had seen carrying the woman. I was stunned at how much he looked like Joe. They could have been brothers or maybe even twins. But the man in the photograph was definitely not Joe.

I turned and grinned at Mom. "It's not Joe," I told her, feeling a relief that was so complete, I almost felt like I could fly. It struck me as amazing that somebody else was walking around who looked so much like Joe and yet probably wasn't even related to him.

Mom came over and looked at the photograph and shook her head. "Well, I'll be. No wonder you thought —" She looked over at Detective Evans. "Sorry. We're just amazed at how strikingly this man resembles somebody we know."

"Really?" Detective Evans said, looking at me. "That's interesting. Were you thinking that the person you know might be the man we've arrested?"

Mom and I looked at each other and then back at Detective Evans. Then we both nodded. I think we were pretty speechless by that time.

"You must be very relieved then," Detective Evans said.

On the way home, Mom suggested that maybe a little celebration was in order for two reasons. One, the police had captured a man who had possibly committed a murder assisted by me, and two, that man wasn't Joe.

We ended up going to the Dairy Queen where Joe and I had done a lot of talking while I suffered under the illusion that he was a murderer. The Dairy Queen seemed like a much friendlier place now that the truth was out.

"We mustn't ever tell Joe that I suspected him," I said, as we sat enjoying a banana split for me and a dish of ice cream for Mom.

"I wouldn't like him to think that I looked at him as a criminal all those times we were together. That might be hard for him to understand."

Mom laughed. "I'm so proud of you helping Detective Evans bring that man to justice. You can't imagine what a wonderful service you have provided to this community, Ryan. I'm just tickled pink. And thank Arnie for me as well. You two make a wonderful team.

I felt so good about Joe not being who I thought he was that I felt like running around the yard and screaming to the whole neighborhood that l had been wrong all the time and my Mom's boyfriend was exactly what he seemed to be: a really nice guy who had not only volunteered a lot of his time taking me places and listening to my complaints but was now an important part of our family.

Now, the only thing I had to worry about was my dad. I was feeling a little guilty about refusing to go with him the last time he had appeared on our doorstep. Neither one of my sisters wanted to go with him and to be truthful, neither did I. Despite that, I knew that he had every right to see us and try to form a relationship, but that was going to be difficult. How did you relate to a father who had deserted his family and then suddenly appears on the scene wanting to pick up where he left off three years earlier?

I was doing my best to try to come to terms with the whole thing but was not having much success. I would like to have talked to Joe about my feelings, but somehow, I didn't think that would be appropriate.

The trial of the man I had seen at the beach whose name was Arthur Holbrook, consumed the news for the next few weeks. It seemed like his picture was everywhere. One night when Joe was over and we were watching TV, he turned to my mom with a smile when Arthur Holbrook's image came onto the TV.

"Who does that guy look like do you think?" he asked with a sly grin on his face.

My mom looked over at me and smiled. "I have no idea," she said.

Both of my sisters giggled. "He looks like you," Angela said. "Only you're much better looking."

"How nice of you to say so," Joe said, blushing slightly.

"I'm relieved that your appearance is the only thing you have in common," Mom said. "And I hope they find him guilty and send him to prison for a long time."

That was the last word we had on the subject and I was relieved that I didn't have to think about it any more.

EPILOGUE

I was a little surprised that my dad never showed up again. Not that I was disappointed. I didn't want anything to do with him and neither did my sisters. But I couldn't help wondering about what he was doing and why he hadn't wanted to see us. I was surprised because he seemed pretty insistent that we go for a ride with him the last time we saw him. I knew that he hadn't gone anywhere because I saw his car now and again as I pedalled around town. I think Mom worried about him showing up again, but she didn't say anything to me. She must have realized that he owned half of our house and that we might have to move if he filed a claim against it.

One afternoon when I was kicking a football around the front lawn with Arnie, a cop car drew up in front of our house and two police officers got out. They nodded at us as they approached our front door.

I wondered if this had something to do with Arthur Coombes. Maybe they had come around to tell us that he had been convicted and sent to jail for life.

Arnie and I looked at each other as Mom opened the front door and the two police officers went inside. We both made a bee-line for the door. There was no way were going to miss out on whatever the cops were about to tell my mom.

"Is this the home of John Sinclair?" I heard one of the officers ask Mom as we entered. They were standing in the hallway and the three of them turned to look at us. Mom nodded her head and pointed toward my room.

"Ryan, why don't you and Arnie go into your room? I don't think this is anything you want to hear?"

She was wrong about that. It was definitely something I wanted to hear. I gestured to Arnie and we headed down the hall toward my room. We stopped before entering and stood listening.

"I'm afraid we have bad news," One of the cops said. There was a long silence before he continued. "Your husband died this morning in the hospital from multiple stab wounds received in a bar last night when he and another man got into an altercation."

"Oh my God," I heard my mom say. "I can't believe it."

Arnie and I went into my room. I sat on my bed and looked out the window. "Poor Mom," I finally said. "It must be a real shock to her."

Arnie stood looking at me without saying anything. It was the first time I could ever remember him being speechless.

When we heard the police officers leave, we went out to the living room. Mom was sitting looking into her hands. She looked about as lost as I had ever seen her. I sat down beside her and put my arm around her.

"Are you okay, Mom?"

She turned to me and attempted a smile. "I guess so, but I just can't help thinking about what a waste. Your dad could have done so much with his life. He had such potential, but he just threw it all away."

Our lives changed a lot after that. Once we all recovered from the initial shock of my dad dying, it seemed like a cloud of despair that had been hanging over us for a long time, suddenly drifted away. We all became less tense, happier, more accepting. Even my two sisters stopped fighting all the time and started treating each other like sisters should. It seemed odd that it took my dad's death to bring us together as a family. Not that we hadn't been a family before, but now there was a closeness that had somehow been previously lacking.

Was it unkind to think ill of our dad? I couldn't help feeling a certain amount of guilt about the way things turned out. I tried to come to terms with it all as best I could, but the guilt lingered. But having a family to fall back on was a wonderful thing. And now that Joe was a real part of our family and my mom seemed happy again, our future looked rosy indeed.

I was glad that I could report to Arnie that at last I had got up the nerve to make a move on Arla. Well, I guess you couldn't call it a move—more like a friendly gesture. I smiled at her and said "good morning". To my surprise, she didn't tell me to get lost or glare at me as though I was hitting on her which was exactly what I was doing. She smiled back and I almost fainted. Since that initial meeting, we've become like real friendly. I haven't asked her out yet, but that's definitely on the agenda—especially since I found out she broke up with that big ox of a boyfriend.

When I told Arnie about my progress, he was over the moon. You would have thought I had won a gold medal at the Olympics—he was that thrilled. It makes a person feel good right down to their toes when he can cause a friend to be that happy. My mom told me that vicarious thrills are sometimes almost as good as the real thing. I guess she's right because Arnie's the living proof.

QUESTIONS ON RYAN'S DILEMMA BY SHARON PARKER

1. Ryan tells his mother what he saw. What details does he leave out? How does he feel after he shares the story with his mother?

2. Three years later this incident still haunts Ryan. Why?

3. What is Ryan's first impression of Joe Swenson? How do Angela and Sara react to Joe Swenson?

4. As Chapter 3 closes, Ryan has spent more time with Joe. What is his impression of Joe?

5. What is Ryan's attitude about his mother's relationship with Joe?

6. In Chapter 7, Mr. Sinclair meets Ryan at school. Why does Ryan say his mom is okay and also disclosed that she has a boyfriend?

7. Arnie provides some comic relief and perspective for Ryan. Tell why you would or would not like Arnie as your best friend.

8. Joe has a key to the house. What does that tell the reader?

9. What is Ryan's dilemma after he and Arnie find the grave? What advice would you give Ryan at this stage?

10. Describe the reaction of Marjorie Sinclair when Ryan shares his "police story". What would you say to Mrs. Sinclair at this point?

ABOUT THE AUTHOR

This is Glenn Parker's 9th novel for young adults. Mr. Parker taught English at secondary schools in both Canada and New Zealand for twenty-five years and has written many short stories published in magazines in both New Zealand and United States during that time. His interests besides writing, include golf, travel, especially cruises, crosswords and reading. He also played hockey for the University of British Columbia in the 60's under Father David Bauer. Many of his novels involve sports such as hockey and baseball, but they always contain an element of conflict within the protagonist's family. The author hopes to continue enjoying cruises and coming up with interesting plots for his novels.

CPSIA information can be obtained
at www.ICGtesting.com
Printed in the USA
LVHW041909180419
614747LV00001B/36